LIGHTS OUT
Book 1

I0589718

By Nathan Reese Maher

1ˢᵗ Edition, July 2015, 2ⁿᵈ Edition, August 2016
3ʳᵈ Edition (Illustrated), August 2017

Cover Art & Illustrations by: Tobias White
Editors: Harley Jacobs

Printed in the United States
ISBN: 9780990320104

All characters, places and monsters are a work of fiction and any resemblance to real life is purely coincidental. This book is intended for entertainment and reading pleasure, none of it is real. Please do not stick needles in your feet to find your soul or to stitch patches on your soul. It doesn't work, I tried it.

Chapter 1

Shelly Wynn, pride of the 8th-grade track team, stood in her backyard. She felt the grass between her feet as she shifted and twirled her body to keep her hula hoop in motion. Her mother used to tell her that she was good at it and that she could compete professionally if she really put her mind to it. She could spin it between her legs, skip with it, twirl it around her neck and transfer it from one arm to the other. Shelly hooped because she enjoyed it, it calmed her whenever she would have an argument or a bad day at school, and it also allowed her to think. Today, she needed to hoop more than ever.

Shelly was worried because something happened that never had happened to her in her thirteen years of life. Somewhere between the moment she fell asleep, to her waking up, all the adults had completely disappeared.

She went over the past week and tried to remember if she had missed an announcement at school, or maybe her mother had said something to her and she forgot.

Shelly looked across her yard, past the treehouse she begged her father to build, and to the opposite side of the alley which separated her house from the neighbors'.

Why didn't they take their cars? She thought as she moved her hips to keep the hoop up.

The robins perched on the power lines and twittered at her as if they shared her confusion regarding the silence of the block. The town only got this quiet when the carnival visited or when the Fighting Raccoons played out of town, but it was still too early in the season.

As she twirled the hoop faster around herself, Shelly failed to notice that the ring began to glow. The harder she thought about her situation the more worried she became. The more anxiety that built inside her, the faster she would make the hoop spin and with each twirl the glow grew brighter and brighter.

She moved the hoop from her waist up to her neck and then around her arms. Shelly was about to switch the ring to her left hand before a voice startled her.

"HELP ME!"

The cry caused her to lose her hoop and it spun off across the yard like a runaway Ferris Wheel. It skittered across the alley, throwing sparks into the air as it struck the gravel and then slammed into the driver's side door of Mr. Martin's car. The window shattered from

3

4

the impact and glass showered both inside and out.

The car alarm echoed through the neighborhood.

Earlier that morning...

The alarm blared, forcing Shelly to abandon her dream of chasing butterflies in a canoe while paddling down a river of chocolate milk. It was just as well, as it was the giraffe's idea anyway and she wasn't making a very good sport of it.

Like every morning, she was wide awake and surging with energy. Today was going to be an amazing day, as it marked the beginning of relay races with her track team. She was pitted against Little-Miss-Perfect, Lydia Gaines, and it was time for her to be put to shame. Everyone knew that Shelly was the better runner, not to mention longer legged. She beat Lydia out by two inches in height and she could make the 100-meter dash in 11.5 seconds. It was Lydia who issued the challenge in front of the entire school and there was no way Shelly was going to back down.

Besides, it was Tuesday and that meant nothing could go wrong. She had gymnastics after school, then dance class with Abby.

Shelly hopped out of bed, opened her bedroom door and immediately headed for the shower. Afterwards, she got dressed, brushed her long black hair, pulled it back into a ponytail, and brushed her teeth. Once ready, she gathered up her backpack, last night's homework and her gym bag before she headed downstairs for breakfast.

The house was unusually quiet. Normally, her mother would have the radio on as she listened to her favorite 90s station. She rounded the stairs and then turned into the kitchen to find it deserted. Every morning at 7 a.m. her mom would be dressed in her business suit, drinking a cup of coffee and cooking one of the Wynn's famous Get-Up-and-Go specials. She had encouraged her mother several times to quit her job and open up her own breakfast diner, but her mother liked her job too much.

"Mom?" Shelly called out to the house.
Nothing.
Maybe her alarm didn't go off? She thought as she walked back upstairs.

She stopped at her parent's bedroom door and rapped softly so as not to startle her.
"Mom, are you awake?"
After no response, she slowly opened the door. Her dad had been out of town on business and wasn't due back until Friday.

Instead of finding her mom sleeping beautifully beneath the covers she found an already made bed. What bothered her most was that her mother's cell phone was still resting on the nightstand.

She looked over the room once more to be certain she hadn't missed anything and returned to the hallway. Shelly didn't have time to look for her mother any further. She had to find something quick to eat before she started out the door. In a few minutes, she would meet Abby at her house so they could walk to school together. It was their morning routine.

Once she returned downstairs to the kitchen, Shelly made herself some toast and jam before putting on her shoes. She went outside and locked the door behind her.

Chapter 2

Shelly raced down the steps to her home and watched her tennis shoes as she went. She looked up as soon as she hit the sidewalk. The concern in her chest increased further as she noted her mother's SUV in the driveway. Her mother always drove to work.

Is mom still in the house? Did she commute? The questions came to her with little answers.

Abigail McMullen, her best friend since kindergarten, lived two blocks away. Shelly was more than eager to explain the weird circumstances surrounding this morning and to talk up the day's future events. Abby wasn't into sports as much as Shelly was. If it weren't for dance class, Abby wouldn't have any exercise at all. Abby had admitted that she only took dance so the two of them could spend more time together.

When Shelly arrived, she found Abby already waiting for her on the porch swing.

"Morning Moon!" Shelly belted out from the stairs.

"Morning Sun." The thirteen-year-old redhead jested as she stood up. She swung her backpack over her shoulder and walked to the stairs to meet her friend.

They greeted each other like this every

morning. It was an inside-reference they shared from a kid's book, "Levity & The Moon Catchers". It was when they first met. The teacher paired them together to read different parts and they really hit it off.

"Are you ready to show Lydia up, today?" Abby asked with enthusiasm.

Shelly put a hand on her hip. "If she decides to show. She may be the team captain of her relay team but popularity isn't going to win her any awards. Especially when she faces against me."

The freckled-faced girl smiled with a nod. "We'll have to celebrate afterwards. Did you want to meet up after ballet today? We could go to your house."

"I'll have to check with my mom. You know how she doesn't like surprise visitors." Shelly replied as Abby walked down the stairs. The two of them started down the sidewalk towards the street. "Speaking of my mom," Shelly turned serious. "She wasn't at home this still in the drive-way.

"Does that seem weird to you?"

"That's totally weird. I mean, who would do that?" Abby asked with sarcasm. "By the way, my parents aren't home either. Who knows, maybe they all snuck off and joined a cult."

She laughed and nudged Abby with her

shoulder. "You read too much."

Abby nudged her back. "You'd be surprised how many people are into those sorts of things. Nancy Drew has encountered things like this before."

"Who?" Shelly asked, suddenly confused.

"Nancy Drew. She's a detective. I've only told you about her a million times. My mom has every book since the 30s."

"How many are there?"

"Close to about 200 of them. I'm on book 32."

"So that's what you do during your free periods." Shelly observed.

"Nothing beats a good book. I hope to have them all read over the summer."

"That's a lot of reading. Do you plan to have any fun at all?" Shelly teased.

"Hey!" Abby pushed Shelly playfully. "There's nothing wrong with reading. It's a lot of fun. You should give it a try."

"I don't know... all those words and page turning. I could hurt myself. Paper cuts cause infections you know."

"Okay, so what do YOU have planned for this summer?"

"I signed up for a summer ballet camp over in Texas. I'll be gone for about a month."

Abby chuckled. "I suppose you and I have different ideas of what fun is."

They rounded the street corner and turned onto Lexington, where several other groups of children were making their way to Applewood Musgrove Middle School, home of the Ferocious Kits. After this year, she'd start cheering for the Raccoons.

Abby pointed farther down the sidewalk where a boy stood clutching his books close to his chest. "There's Lochan Hayre. I feel kind of sorry for him."

Shelly leaned in to whisper. "Why do you say that?"

"He transferred here a month ago. He hasn't made any friends yet."

"Really? No one?"

"No one." Abby repeated. "I hear his parents were from somewhere in India."

"I wonder what India is like?" Shelly mused aloud.

As they approached, Abby touched Shelly's arm. "I'm going to talk to him."

"Abby wait—" She tried to warn in whisper but was cut off.

"—Hi! Lochan, right?"

The kid was downtrodden. His eyes slowly raised and suddenly he was surprised that someone was speaking to him. He was smaller than most other boys and skinny. He clutched his books tighter against his chest and he looked around just to be sure she wasn't talking to someone else.

"Yes? – Ah, what is it?" He replied with a thick accent.

"How have you been?" Abby asked with hopes of putting him at ease.

"Not good." He shuffled a foot behind him.

"Is something wrong?" She asked as she scrunched her eyebrows and tilted her head.

"Everything is wrong. You know why, don't pretend that you don't." He shook his head as if trying to clear away a thought and then broke into a run, careful to dodge around them.

"Hey!" Abby called after him. "Where are you going?" She pointed in the direction they were heading. "The school is this way."

"And that is why he has no friends." Shelly observed jokingly.

Abby sighed. "I don't know." She paused as she watched him disappear down the street. "He looked afraid of something."

"He's probably afraid of people, or maybe he gets scared around girls. I hear that's a thing." Shelly reasoned.

"A thing?" Abby threw a confused glare at her darker-skinned bestie.

Shelly shrugged. "You know, like a psychosis or something."

"Maybe..." Abby squinted her eyes to see if she could find him in the distance. "I don't know."

She repositioned her backpack on her shoulders. "Come on, we don't want to be late."

When they reached the school, all the 6th through 8th graders collected around the front doors.

"That's strange." Abby announced between them. "Is there something wrong? Why isn't anyone going inside?"

Shelly looked around and spotted a few of their fellow classmates peering into the windows of Ms. Schumacher's classroom, while others attempted to see past the blinds of the front office windows.

"It looks like no one can get in." Shelly stated with bewilderment.

Shelly spied a trustworthy face in the sea of children and pulled Abby with her to meet up. Wendy Freeman was waiting with her instrument case alongside a few of her bandmates.

"Wendy? What's the scoop?" Shelly asked.

"The doors are locked." She replied grimly. The long raven-haired girl shifted in her Mary Jane shoes. "The parking lot is empty too."

"What do you mean the parking lot is empty?" Shelly demanded. "Where are all the teachers?"

"Don't know." Replied Wendy as she knocked the tip of her shoe three times on the pavement. "Do you know if we're supposed to have school today? Maybe the teachers forgot to tell us."

Abby and Shelly look at one another and shrugged.

"I don't think so. Relays start today. Mrs. Burgeon had us pick teams yesterday. She was very sure we'd compete today." Shelly explained confidently.

Wendy also shrugged. "I was supposed to have early morning practice with Mr. Dayton. I've been here for over an hour. He didn't mention anything about a delay."

"Is this a joke?" Abby asked, a bit disturbed. "Because I don't find this very funny."

A boy flautist spoke up from Wendy's close circle of friends. "A lot of kids' parents weren't home this morning and now the teachers are missing."

Abby and Shelly looked to each other in silent confirmation.

"Our parents weren't home either." Shelly voiced with concern.

Wendy's face brightened. "If the teachers aren't here and our parents aren't here then that just means one thing." She announced it as loudly as she could. "No school today!"

She quickly snatched up her instrument case. "Come on guys." She encouraged her friends. "No school today."

"Wait – don't you think we should—" Abby was interrupted by the chanting of another classmate.

"No school today!"

Another took up the cheer. "No school today!"

Soon, all the children were chanting it. "No school! No school!"

The idea of not having to attend class was very appealing to Shelly, especially if it meant having the full day to herself. Despite it all, something gnawed at her about the situation that wasn't quite right.

"Hey, gloomy face." Abby teased. "This is a good thing right? You can trounce Lydia tomorrow."

The school bell rang and all the children grew silent. All eyes focused on the doors, waiting for some sign of a teacher or faculty member to realize their mistake and unlock the doors. Everyone looked for that individual to wave them in and apologize for not letting them in sooner.

No one came.

The bell droned on and many felt that familiar tug to race to their respective classrooms, lest they be punished for being tardy. The doors remained locked and the school remained still. Once the bell finally ceased, a breath of relief swept through the kids. Everyone hastily left, giddy that they could enjoy the day.

Abby turned back to Shelly. "It's good to have a day off, right? So why does it feel so eerie?"

"Remember what Lochan said? Something is very wrong, Abby."

"Walk back with me?" Abby pleaded as she tried to shake the spooky feeling that came over them.

"Sure." Shelly agreed.

Once they put enough distance between themselves and the school, Abby broke the unusual silence between them.

"The most messed up thing about this is that I was looking forward to you defeating Lydia. If anyone deserves to be put in their place it's her. Just the other day she bumped into me on purpose and then made a scene about how I bumped into her. Don't even get me started on how a week before that she offered me concealer for my freckles in front of her misfit entourage. There is nothing wrong with freckles."

"Don't let her get to you. She's mean to everyone. Some people are just unhappy until they ruin someone else's day." Shelly advised in sympathy.

After another period of silence and several blocks later they arrived at the McMullen residence.

"Home again, home again." Abby sighed as she started up the stairs to her porch. "I'm going to do some reading while I wait for my parents to get home. Wait until they hear how there was no school today, they will flip. Give me a call when your mom comes home to see if it would still be all right for me to come over afterwards, okay?"

Shelly gave her the thumbs up and replied, "Happy reading."

Chapter 3

Presently...

The car alarm continued to announce her vandalism to the entire town. Shelly's first reaction was to run, but it was her hoop after all and everyone would know she was the one who did it. She drew closer to see if there was any way for her to fix it.

Somehow her hula hoop had cut into the driver's side door like the vehicle was made of cheese. The metal was still glowing red, but the hoop itself appeared unscathed. Glass was everywhere.

She quickly tapped the hoop with her fingers to test if it was hot but found that it was no different in temperature than when she had been playing with it. With a quick tug she was able to free it, revealing the intensity of the gash.

"No way." She whispered to herself as she turned the hoop over in her hands.

Naturally, she spun the hoop around her wrists, keeping the ring in front of her. Just as before, her hula-hoop began to glow, small at first, yet it glowed brighter the faster it spun. She stopped it before grew too bright in fear of it slipping from her hand again.

What if this time it cut down a telephone pole or went into someone's home? She thought.

"Help me!" Demanded the voice again and this time a ripple of pain swept through her chest followed by the familiar bite of dread.

Her ears clogged up as if she had just gotten water in them and there was a slight inner ringing that blocked the sound of the world around her. She knew where it came from, almost as if it were instinctual. The cry came from the park.

The voice was small but strong, as if a tiny child spoke into a megaphone right into her ear. Shelly clutched onto her hoop and sprinted towards the cry.

The plea sounded desperate and full of fear. It echoed inside her long after the voice had dissipated. Shelly ran as quickly as she could, with her tennis shoes striking the pavement in rapid succession. She could feel the air push against her as it blew through her hair. She moved quickly, faster than she had ever moved before, and it felt like each time her foot pushed against the ground that the ground would push back and send her bounding.

She was beyond the alleyway, down the side street and several blocks away before she noticed the same glow from her hoop emanating from her shoes. Fearful of putting herself in danger, she made an abrupt stop.

Her feet skidded against the concrete sidewalk and it cracked beneath her as if struck by a powerful sledge hammer.

"It's not the hoop." She said aloud as she watched the light diminish from her shoes. She looked between them and then to her hand. "It's me." A grin grew across her face.

She returned to her run. Shelly kept one eye on her shoes as they regained their previous illumination. She felt as if she could leap into the air and sail for miles. Then she missed the entrance to the park and had to slow herself, as not to harm anything, before turning back around.

Willow Park was fit with swings, a slide, a merry-go-round and a few other plastic playsets. There were benches and small brick paths that led around the gardens. There was also the giant willow tree from where she imagined the park got its name. Shelly remembered how her and her friends used to climb it for hours.

It wasn't hard for Shelly to spot the source of the cry. A small boy, maybe five years old and fairly tan was trapped at the top of the slide. He kicked out his legs and kept looking around trying to find someone to help him. Besides the two of them the park was empty.

"You have to be kidding me." She muttered to herself. "I ran all the way here for this?"

She yelled, "Hey, do you need help?"

The boy was surprised to see her. He reached out, frantically opening and closing his hands as if it would draw her nearer. He didn't say anything outside of a few grunts and squeals.

She sighed and walked over to the slide. When she reached its base, she called up to him. "Are you too scared to come down?"

He squealed more, as if something had stolen his tongue. He reached out to her more, making an "ee" sound as he stretched out his arms.

She walked around to the ladder and paused to look up at him.

The ground began to shake as she debated on what was the best way to coax him. Shelly wavered while she struggled to keep her balance. Then the soil slipped from beneath her feet. Frightened that she would be sucked in, Shelly leaped to the first rung and clamored partly up the ladder. The ground crumbled around them into a hollow underground chasm where hundreds of feet below ran rivers of lava. Hot air blew up and got caught like a web in her hair. It smelled strongly of matches.

"Oh my gosh!" She cried out. "What's happening? What is happening!?" Shelly clutched the railing and wove her free arm around it to ensure she didn't plummet into the abyss.

The little boy peeked over the top, the fear in his eyes danced with the heat below. He then was startled by something out of the deep and he gave out a high-pitched scream.

Shelly dared to look over the railing and she was overwhelmed by the horror of it. It was a hound, taller than any dog she had ever seen; almost the size of a deer. It had long skinny legs, red fur and flames licked from its back. Its jaw hung wide, revealing sharp jagged teeth with a tongue that slinked out the side with drool.

The fiery beast lumbered from the nightmare below, leapt upon outcropped rocks and it tiptoed along the rocky ledges. The creature stared at her with hungry eyes.

"Stay away!" Shelly screamed.

The hound did not stop.

Shelly climbed farther up the ladder. "Get away!" She yelled again, but the beast continued to climb.

She and the little boy were trapped and it was only a matter of time before it descended upon them. The boy cried over their doomed fate. His tears flowed down his face in streams.

Shelly's hand tightened around her hoop. She remembered what she did to her neighbor's car and realized that she had the means to save them both. She only had one shot.

The teenager planted her feet firmly on the step and bent her knees to save her balance. Then, she began to twirl her hoop, first between her hands, then to her wrists and down her arm. As the hoop spun, it gained in a color as a hum pulsed between rotations. Once it took to a brilliant white she slung the hoop towards the monster.

It missed.

Chapter 4

Just by a few inches, the hoop skittered past the horror, causing it to bounce off the grass like a rock across a pond. A yelp came from the tiny terrier as it was afraid of being hit. No longer a gigantic beast with blazing flames and evil eyes, the tiny white dog retreated as the park returned to its previous state. Where once there was the deep underground with rivers of lava was now a freshly cut lawn. Everything was exactly as it had been the moment she arrived.

Shelly breathed a sigh of relief and the small boy buried his face into her shirt. His hands opened and closed around her waist as he sniffed from the previous tears. Shelly hugged him back, relieved that it was over. From over her shoulder she watched as the miniature dog made its way across the playground. It let out a few protests, before continuing on its way.

Once it disappeared out on the street, she released her hug. "What are you doing here?"

He sniffed again. He glanced about the park before looking back to her. He pats the railing of the slide.

"Where are you parents?" It was a habitual question. One that had been ingrained in her from her TV shows. She later guessed that he was in the same situation as everyone else.

His brown eyes twinkled and his face scrunched to reveal a saddened lip.

"Your mom and dad are gone too, huh?"

The child nodded and wiped his eyes.

"Do you have anyone here? A brother or maybe a sister?"

He nodded his little head and pointed toward the street, then opened and closed his hands repeatedly as he had done before, as if trying to reach for something far away.

"Okay – well, why don't you show me where you live so we can find someone to take care of you."

The kid continued to look at her but didn't budge.

"Come on, let's go find your brother or sister. Do you want to slide down?"

He shook his head and reached out for her again.

Shelly sighed. "You want us to go down together?"

He hesitated but then nodded his head in agreement.

"Okay then." Shelly climbed the rest of the way up the slide and tried her best to maneuver around him so that she could position him between her legs. Shelly then wrapped her arms around him snuggly. "You ready?"

The child grabbed her hands and held them tightly.

"Three... two... one—" She pushed off.

Hand-in-hand, the two of them walked down the sidewalk on Wormwood Drive. The streets were empty aside from parked cars and the chirping of birds. Shelly clutched her hula hoop now on her shoulder and kept it close in case she encountered any more demon-dogs.

She breathed in the spring air and let it soothe her nerves. Her hands quivered slightly from the memory of the heat and the creature that stalked them from below. She didn't know if it had been real or if she was losing her mind. Was the world unraveling? Did the dog create it? Did the boy?

This day just kept getting weirder and weirder.

The boy stopped before the end of the fence, just shy of where the sidewalks met. He tugged on her arm and she stopped.

"What?" Shelly demanded, slightly annoyed by the sudden jolt.

The boy said nothing but instead continued to stand, staring ahead without a peep. He was steadfast. His hair shifted in the breeze.

"We can't just stop, we have to keep go—"

A pair of kids on their mountain bikes zoomed by from the obscured street.

"Coming through!" A blonde boy called out as he jumped off the sidewalk and onto the street.

The boy looked back and she could see his face. She didn't recognize him from class. He returned her gaze and his eyes flashed red. He continued to pedal in order to keep up with his friend and returned his attention back to his destination.

"Well that was rude." She said to herself. She hesitantly asked, "Did you know they were coming?"

He shrugged his shoulders and then pulled her farther down the street. The kid was beginning to scare her.

In time, they reached his home, which was a one-story house with a yellow front porch and a screen door. The front yard was decorated with lawn gnomes that resided next to a birdbath windmill. There were a few plastic chairs scattered about the porch and a set of wind chimes, which hung above the welcome mat, clinked in the breeze.

Shelly walked the boy up the steps and knocked on the screen door. It didn't take long before a pudgy pacific islander opened the front door. She appeared to be two grades above her and wore a bright yellow dress.

"Mahalo for bringing Ioane back." The girl

29

expressed no sense of relief and held herself quite calm. "I warned him not to go. I told him the boogieman would catch him and eat him with brussel sprouts. He never listens though." She sighed. "Where was he this time?"

Ioane let go of Shelly's hand and went inside without even a look back.

"He was in the park. I found him at the top of the slide. He was screaming for help. He probably got scared being all alone." Shelly explained.

"That's very odd. Ioane is never scared of the slide even though I tell him that if he goes down too fast he'll travel to a different dimension and we'll never see him again."

"That's a frightening thing to say to your brother." Shelly observed while mildly disturbed.

"Do you have a brother?"

"Um," Shelly shook her head. "Only child."

"If you had a brother you would probably say the same things. Anyway..." she sighed. "I don't think it was Ioane that was screaming. He hasn't said a word since our parents went missing. They probably were kidnapped by the mafia."

"How long have your parents been missing?"

"Since this morning." She sighed again. "Although last time they left, Ioane didn't

31

speak for an entire month. They were visiting family in Lanai... so they said."

"Don't take this the wrong way," Shelly tried to reassure. "But you're a very strange person. How come I haven't seen you at school?"

"Not strange, just different." She looked to the side. "I'm taught at home. I don't go to normal school. It's the best way to avoid alien mind control. At least that is what my father says."

"My name is Shelly Wynn, by-the-way."

"Aloha, I'm Haukea. I don't expect you to remember it."

Shelly tilted her head slightly with confusion. "Why wouldn't I remember it?"

Haukea shrugged her shoulders. "It's a different name. Not like Sarah or Jennifer. Most people don't. If it helps, just think of ways I can ruin your day."

"How?"

"How-key-ya, your car." She paused. "Just kidding."

Shelly thumbed to the street behind her. "I think I'm going to go."

Haukea nodded at her shoulder. "You hoop? You any good?"

With confidence Shelly declared, "The best!"

"Maybe I'll see you hoop one day. If your

heart doesn't stop."

"Are you threatening me?"

"People in the United Kingdom used to go to the doctor for hurting their spine and others died because their heart stopped. It was because of hooping too much."

"I don't think that's true." Shelly combated as she gripped her hoop. "I'll see you later." She said as she took a step back.

Haukea shrugged her shoulders. "Mahalo again for bringing Ioane home alive." She waved, curtsied awkwardly and then closed the door.

"Wow..." Shelly muttered. She turned and struck out on the sidewalk. "That girl is something else." She said as she made her way back home.

As Shelly rounded the street, Haukea watched her go from a crack in a fence, already one block from where Shelly had previously seen her.

Shelly hurried home. She had enough mystery and excitement for one day. Besides, who could say that her mom hadn't returned? She would have to explain why there wasn't any school today. She couldn't wait until Abby would come over so she could tell her everything she's encountered thus far. How will she explain the park without sounding like a crazy person?

When she arrived at home she expected to be assaulted with a whirlwind of questions, but the sound of the front door wasn't enough to rouse anyone inside.

"Mom? I'm home!" Shelly called out.

The house remained silent.

As before, Shelly checked the likely rooms her mother would be in, but still no luck. She then went to the kitchen and made herself some lunch. With sandwich in-hand she moved to the living room, plopped on the couch and clicked the remote to turn on the TV. The first channel was filled with static. She tried the other cable channels but they too were snowy.

"What's wrong now?"

She remembered all those times her father messed with it. Most of those times ended with frustration and him inevitably calling the cable company to send someone out. It's not something she wanted to mess with right now. She switched the TV to receive only the local channels. What she found there disturbed her. Instead of the usual shows, it displayed a "Stand By" screen accompanied by a long droning noise.

Shelly got worried. She wondered how Abby was doing, if her parents had returned or if she had received any calls with updates.

Shelly's mom was very strict when it came to cell phones.

"You're young and don't need to be one of those girls who spends her life tweeting and texting."

Abby had one though.

She went to the kitchen and lifted the phone off the receiver. With a growing nervousness, she dialed Abby's number. It took four rings before someone picked up.

"Hello?" It was good to hear Abby's voice.

"Hey Abby, this is Shelly." She replied. "Have your parents come back yet?"

"No, not yet. They usually work until five anyway. How about your mom?"

"No – she works until five too, but I was hoping she came back home for lunch like she always does."

"I'm sure it's nothing to worry about." Abby reassured.

"Does your cable work?"

"I don't know, I haven't tried it."

Shelly sighed and peeked back into the living room. "It's just static now and the local channels are displaying that 'stand by' picture. This type of stuff only happens in the movies when something bad has happened."

"I'm sure someone will fix it. If you are bored you can try reading or something."

"I don't know..." Shelly trailed.

35

"How?" Abby interrupted. "It's easy. Just take it slow. First you pick up the book and then you open the front cover."

"Ha ha – very funny." She paused. "I think I might lie down. A lot of things have happened today and I'm a little overwhelmed."

"Oh? Like what?"

"I can't tell you over the phone. It's something I need to tell you in person."

"Ah – it must be serious. I'll give you call as soon as my parents are home, okay?"

"Okay—" Shelly took a breath. "I'll talk with you later then."

"Have a nice nap." Abby disconnected the call.

Taking a nap sounded like the best option for her right now. She took the wireless with her to her bedroom, took off her shoes and climbed into her bed. It didn't take long to fall asleep.

She went down the stairs from her bedroom and into the kitchen. The smell of bacon called her to the island where she took a seat on a stool. Her mother turned around with a spatula in hand and a crackling pan in the other.

"Eat up, sweetheart, you looked famished."

She scraped the empty pan of grease onto the island counter and a plate with two sunny side up eggs, three strips of bacon and four slices of toast appeared in front of her. There wasn't any silverware.

"Thanks, mom." She bit into a slice of toast.

The pan and spatula then vanished from her mother's hands. She untied her apron and neatly folded it. Her mom handed it to her.

"Make sure you take a flashlight. You know she'll be scared in the dark."

When Shelly took it, the apron was gone and so too was her breakfast. In its place was the flashlight.

She then tilted her head as if trying to escape from a thought. "Wait... mom?"

Her mom was gone, leaving behind an empty kitchen.

"Where are you?" Shelly called out.

The kitchen phone rang!

Shelly's eyes snapped open. Her bedroom was dark with only the lights from the streetlamps filtering in through her blinds. She sat up and looked around. Her head felt heavy and muddled.

Chapter 5

The phone rang again.

Shelly blinked a few times and rubbed her face before picking up the phone.

She hit the answer button. "Hello?"

"Shelly?"

It was Abby again.

"Uh-huh?" She replied sleepily.

"You sound tired, did I wake you up?"

"Yea, but no big." She paused groggily. "What time is it?"

"It's 8:30. Listen, my parents haven't come back yet. I tried calling their work but the phone just rings. Can I come over?"

"I can't believe I slept that long. Sorry, I must have been really tired." Shelly said as she shifted her head back and forth to shake out the fog.

"Don't worry about it. I-I'll be over in a few."

They hung up at the same time.

Shelly stretched and slowly got out of bed. She turned on the lights as she went down to the ground floor. The rest of the house was also black. Normally her mother would have a few lights on in the kitchen and the living room. Even if she had gone to bed she would have at least left the hallway bathroom light on for Shelly. Her mom had been doing it since Shelly was three.

She kept poking her head into each room she passed, just in case, but knew deep down that just like Abby's parents, her mother wasn't going to be home.

Her stomach growled. Maybe that's why she dreamed of breakfast. If she had the money she would order a pizza. Given the circumstances, she didn't think her mother would have minded. Maybe Abby was hungry too and she could help her decide what to make.

She went into the kitchen and examined the cabinets hoping for some inspiration. Shelly's eyes then rested on the utility drawer where the flashlight was stored.

"Just in case," she uttered to herself. She pulled the flashlight from its home and placed it on the counter where her plate had been served in the dream.

The doorbell rang.

Way too soon for Abby to be here, Shelly approached the front door with caution. "Who is it?"

"Come on, Shell – it's me." Came Abby's voice.

Still confused by how quickly Abby had arrived, she opened the door to the backpack toting red-head.

"That was fast." Shelly observed as her

friend hastily came inside.

"I was already on my way when I called. I figured that you wouldn't say no."

"Right..." Shelly mused. "You have a cellphone."

"Is your mum back?" Abby asked with concern.

Shelly wrapped her arms around her for comfort. "Not yet. She's never been gone this long without telling me."

"My dad comes straight home from work. Then there is the whole thing with the teachers missing. I've been watching the street and I haven't seen any cars. I saw a few kids, but no adults. I'm starting to get freaked out." Her voice had a touch of the shakes.

"That's not the half of it. There are a few other strange things that have been happening too." Shelly added.

"Like what exactly?"

Shelly inhaled deeply to gather courage. "You wouldn't believe me if I told you. You-you're going to have to follow me outside for a moment."

Shelly grabbed the flashlight from the kitchen and took Abby to her backyard.

The alley lights shone on the street but shadows gripped her neighbor's car like it was cursed. She dragged Abby within a few feet of it and then shown the flashlight on the driver's side door.

"Holy beans, what happened?!" Abby's eyes were wide with disbelief.

Shelly bit her lip. "I did it." She sighed.

Abby blinked, still shocked. "How?"

"I lost control of my hoop and it went sailing across the alley and into the car door. The metal was really hot, almost as if the hoop was a thousand degrees."

"Your... hula hoop did this?"

"Since this morning, whenever I spin my hoop it glows. I don't know how exactly. It just does."

"Show me!" Abby demanded with piqued interest.

"What?" Now it was Shelly's turn to be shocked. This wasn't quite the reaction she expected.

"Show me!" Abby begged. "I want to see you make it glow. Can you do it again?"

Shelly stepped back. "I don't know if that's a good idea."

"Well..." Abby crossed her arms dramatically over her chest. "If you think you can't do it."

Abby was trying to pressure her. Shelly knew the Wynn reputation was on the line. She gave in, as she had so many times before. "Fine – If you get cut in half it's not my

41

fault."

"Then just don't throw it at me." Abby protested in jest.

Shelly went back inside and grabbed her hoop, only to return shortly after where Abby was waiting for her.

"You could have left me with the flashlight, you know." Abby whimpered a little.

Shelly shook her head and made sure she had plenty of space so that she wouldn't hit anything. As many times before, she kept the hoop close to her waist and then twirled it with small, tight bursts of speed. As the hoop gathered in momentum it gave off a hum that took on a light blue illumination far brighter than the streetlamps. It was so bright, that it lit up the entire backyard.

Shelly stopped it before it got out of control and the light slowly dimmed, putting the two of them back into darkness.

Abby cupped her hands over her mouth then, as if her excitement was too much for her, she dropped her hands and let out a squeal. "That is so freaking awesome! I mean – like – WOW! I-I-believed you before but I didn't believe-you-believe-you." She nearly jumped out of her shoes. "When you lost it, the hoop, it cut into the car?!" She pointed at the damage. "Are you serious? Do you know what this means?"

"No." Shelly replied with cold uncertainty. "No I don't."

Abby waved her arms in front of her. "I don't either, but now I'm not the only one. I can do something too!" She dropped her backpack on the ground before Shelly could even say anything. Abby opened her pack and pulled out a Nancy Drew book and clutched it tightly against herself.

Shelly's eyebrows lowered. "What do you mean?"

Abby held the book out in front of her. "Just watch."

Small motes of light danced about her book. With that, she released the book and it floated in the air; drifting like they had seen in a documentary about living in space. The motes soon extinguished themselves but the book kept floating.

Shelly was speechless.

Abby poked the binding and the book rotated while levitating above the ground, spinning with the slightest of movement.

"What are you doing?" Shelly demanded with her mouth slightly agape.

Abby shrugged and shook her head with a smile. "I don't know, but watch this." She focused on the book intensively and her face scrunched up. "Stop!" Just as the word came out of her mouth the book froze in place while

suspended in the air.

Abby pushed against it and it didn't budge.

"It won't move. You can even climb on it and it won't go anywhere." She gave it a few additional pushes before giving up entirely.

Shelly placed her hand on it and gave it a light nudge. "This is both cool and disturbing."

"I know! I'm so excited. Now I can read on my back without the blood running out of my fingers."

"Can you do other things instead of books?"

"Of course, I can. Here, give me your flashlight."

Shelly held out the flashlight like it were a relay baton. As Abby reached out to grab it, the alley lights, as well as those from the house and surrounding neighborhood, shut off. They were left in complete darkness.

Abby whimpered. "What's happening?"

"The power shut off." Shelly clicked on the flashlight.

"But it's not storming out." Abby's face was lit by the beam. "This is normally when the killer comes out of hiding and does someone in."

"We're not in one of your detective stories, Abby." Shelly gazed about the neighborhood. "Looks like no one else's lights are on either. This is bad."

"This is worse than bad, Shell." Abby's

voice was shaky and growing softer by the moment. "All the adults are gone. Who's going to turn the lights back on if there isn't anyone to fix it?"

"I'm sure the adults will be back soon." Shelly said with uncertainty as she scanned her backyard with the flashlight.

"I'm afraid they're not coming." Abby said fearfully. "Our parents, our teachers – everyone! They've disappeared. That's it. Lights out, Shelly. We're on our own. My parents have never disappeared like this – neither has anyone else's. What are we going to do?"

"Calm down, Abby." Shelly hoped that if she pretended to be brave that she could shake how frightened she was becoming. She wasn't going to quit though, especially not since things got harder. That's not the Wynn way. "Think of all the other kids out there who are also scared. We should go check on everyone and see if they are okay."

Abby looked around them and cringed. Every little thing seemed to take on a sinister appearance, the lamp posts, the trees, the bushes – everything.

"Do you think that is best? I mean, what if we run into a crazed lunatic or something. This is how it starts, you know? Psychopaths love it when it's dark and terrifying outside."

"If there are any psychos out there then we can ask if they know where our parents are. I don't think that's something we'll have to worry about. Besides, most psychos are adults anyways."

Abby appeared less on edge. "Still though, we don't know what's going on. It may not be safe for us to go out right now. It may be better if we just go inside."

"Just think how terrified you are right now and imagine you being seven-years-old or even younger. How scared would you be? We should at least check with everyone on the block." She clutched her hula hoop and suddenly got an idea. "Think of it like an adventure. How often do we get to do things like this?"

"I know what you're trying to do, Shell. You're just trying to make me feel better. I read mysteries because I'm too scared to go out and have adventures myself. I'm scared of the dark, you know?"

"Don't worry, it's just a few houses. What possibly could go wrong?"

"Besides our parents disappearing and then learning that I can make things float and stop in mid-air and you can cut open cars with your hula hoop? Well... that part is pretty cool."

"See? If it'll make you feel better, I have another flashlight that you can use. We'll just check the street and then see how we're doing then before branching out."

"There's no talking you out of this, is there?" Abby whined.

"I'm afraid not. Come on. It'll be fun." She reassured.

Shelly turned back towards the house and focused the light where she was going to walk. She didn't take more than a few steps before Abby cried out in pain.

Shelly spun around and shown the light back on her friend. Abby was next to her book rubbing her forehead.

She laughed at herself. "Ow-ow-ow..."

"What happened?"

Abby sniffed with self-pity. "I hit my head on my book." She held it up. "I got it now."

"Oh – I'm sorry. I guess I should have made sure you were ready."

"It's okay. It's not every day that you have to deal with a flying book." She picked up her backpack and hefted it over her shoulder. She sighed. "Let's get this over with."

Chapter 6

Together, Shelly and Abby walked down the street with their flashlights knocking on the door of every house they encountered. The first two homes offered no answer. It was expected. As far as Shelly knew, there weren't any children living there.

When they reached the third home belonging to the Mendoza's, their son answered the door. He was only eight.

He kept a brave face. "Hello."

"Hi there. I'm Shelly Wynn. I live three houses down. I'm just checking to see if everyone is okay."

He looked her up and down and then behind her where her friend stood.

"Oh—" Shelly apologized. "This is Abby McMullen. She's my best friend."

"Aw." Abby smiled at her comment. "Hello." She waved back.

"We're okay." He responded quietly.

A girl's voice called at him harshly from deeper inside the house. "¿Quién es?"

"La vecina." He called back.

Shelly blinked her eyes a couple of times with confusion. "Are your parents gone too?"

The boy nodded his head.

"If you need anything you can come over to my house, okay? Number 417."

The boy nodded his head again and closed the door without saying a word. They both heard something exchanged in Spanish but couldn't tell beyond that.

"Someone is a little shy." Abby commented.

"He's probably been told not to speak to strangers." Shelly remarked as she walked down the steps of the front porch. "Do you know what he said?"

"You mean the head nodding?" She joked.

"No – genius, the other parts."

Abby laughed. "Someone asked who it was and he said the neighbor. Aren't you taking Spanish?"

"No, I switched to German at the last minute."

They rounded the sidewalk and continued onto the next house.

"Why did you switch to German?"

"Because I heard that they have better food days and I don't like beans."

"How can you not like beans? It's like a staple."

"I just don't. I think it's a texture thing."

"That's weird."

"Says the girl who doesn't like broccoli."

"I'm sorry, I can't help but feel like I'm killing tiny trees—"

Abby is interrupted by a child's scream

from the house across the street. The two exchanged a look to validate what they had heard and then ran towards it.

The scream continued as they rushed up the sidewalk, jumped a couple of stairs and reached the front door. Shelly tried the doorknob but it was locked.

Panicked, Shelly pounded on the door. "Hello?! Do you need help? Hello!?"

Abby searched around the various potted plants on the porch among other assorted things. "Help me look around to see if there is a key." She commanded.

Shelly stretched to check the top frame of the door and then lifted the welcome mat she had been standing on. Beneath it was a small brass key.

She snatched it up and showed it to her partner in crime. "Got it!"

"That's a terrible place to hide a key!" Abby stressed as she brushed her dirty hands on her jeans. "It took us like 15 seconds to find it."

Shelly shakily forced the key into the lock and turned the bolt aside. As she pushed past the door the scream came again. This time it came from a back room.

"We're here!" Shelly yelled as she ran inside the dark house. "We're coming."

The two of them passed the living room,

ran down a hallway and then stopped at a
closed door. Shelly burst inside to see a small
boy with a flashlight huddled in the corner of
his room. He wore star pajamas.

They were struck with disbelief as they
stumbled onto a fight between a small stuffed
rabbit waving its wooden sword at an equally
sized stuffed alligator who snapped its jaws
at each swing.

The little boy pointed to the battle.
"Please help Percy!"

Shelly frantically looked about and spotted
a blanket across the room on the bed. She

squeezed against the wall to avoid the ensuring battle.

The alligator lunged at the rabbit and it barely dodged out of the way. For its trouble, the stuffed alligator received a thump on the head by the rabbit's sword.

Abby pointed to the aggressive toy and strongly commanded, "Up!" and the reptile weightlessly lifted off the ground and floated towards the ceiling.

"Great carrots and cabbage," declared the brown rabbit. "That's not something you see every day." Without missing a second, he sheathed his sword in his belt and hopped into the boy's arms who hugged him close.

"We're saved, Percy!" The boy giggled joyously.

"Oh." Shelly remarked as she abandoned her pursuit of the blanket. It's too bad, she looked forward to capturing it.

The alligator tried to move its legs to escape but instead it only ended up turning upside down. As soon as it reached the ceiling, Abby commanded it to stop and the creature froze in place.

"Well," Abby shrugged her shoulders innocently. "When you have an ability, use it."

Shelly shone her light on the boy. "Are you okay?"

"You bet I am!" Replied the child excitedly

as he got off the ground.

The rabbit leaped from his hands and onto the floor. "Many thanks, good ladies for your assistance. I am Sir Perceval Rabbit but please call me Percy. Behind me is my dearest friend, Thomas Haines LeRue."

"Shelly? I thought I was just hearing things before, but did you just hear what I heard?" Abby begged to confirm her sanity.

Her friend nodded her head in the glow of the room. "A talking rabbit?"

"Uh-huh. Um..." Abby fumbled with her words and swallowed to clear them out. "Ah – Hello, Sir Rabbit."

Percy nodded with understanding as one of his ears dropped against his head. "You are as surprised as I was... Miss?"

"Abby." She replied.

"And I'm Shelly. I live down the street."

"A pleasure to make your acquaintance. We surely would have met our ends had not the two of you come to the rescue. For that, you have our gratitude."

Thomas pointed to the ceiling. "How did you do that?"

Abby shrugged. "I'm not sure. It just started happening today. Probably the same way Percy and the alligator came to life."

Shelly turned to the brown-haired boy. "Thomas, do you have anyone here to take care of you? Like a brother or a sister?"

"No, just me and Percy."

"I'm assuming your parents are missing too?" Shelly asked with concern.

He nodded. "Since this morning. Normally, my mom takes me to school but I haven't been able to find her."

The brown rabbit looked up to his child and then to Shelly. "Do you know where they might have gone?"

Shelly shook her head. "Everyone's parents are missing."

"When will they be back?" Thomas asked with a bit of shakiness in his voice.

Shelly pleaded to Abby with her eyes for some help.

"I'm sure they'll turn up soon." Abby readdressed Thomas and Percy. "Do you have any friends or family? Someone maybe close in age?"

"Umm..." He hesitated. "I have cousins across town, but they won't answer their phone."

Abby turned back to Shelly. "What do you think?"

Shelly cast her flashlight into every corner of the room. She paused in thought. "I think he'd be better off with his family than all alone." The rabbit's ears straightened. "All alone with Percy that is."

"I wholeheartedly agree with you, Lady Shelly. When shall we embark?" Asked the rabbit.

"Do you or Thomas know where his cousins are?" Shelly asked with hope.

The rabbit conceded to Thomas as he inquired silently with his tiny button eyes.

"Of course, I do!" Thomas laughed. "I ride my bike there all the time. Sir Perceval and I get invitations to tea parties."

"Okay." Shelly agreed. "Do you have an overnight bag? We'll help you pack."

Chapter 7

The three of them set their kickstands for their bikes and leaned them against the sidewalk outside the gigantic mansion in Cherrywood Terrace.

The ride was difficult in the dark, if not spooky. Normally at this time of night the town would be alive with activity. Tonight, it seemed like everyone was hiding under their covers.

Despite the shadows that lurked behind them, the mansion provided them a beacon of hope as all the lights still shown despite the blackout.

"Are you sure this is the place?" Shelly asked as she took in its size.

"This is a really big house." Abby added in awe. "Your cousin lives here?"

Thomas giggled. "Yup! I come here all the time." He unslung his backpack and eased it to the ground to allow Percy to leap out of the pouch.

"Many times have the three of us sat down to tea. Lee-dee is a fantastic hostess." Perceval announced as he adjusted his belt.

Shelly insisted that she bring her hula hoop with her, just in case they needed it. She checked it on her shoulder and then turned off her flashlight.

57

"Why are the lights still on?" Shelly asked out of curiosity.

Abby shined her light up to the roof. "Solar panels. I saw them as we rode up. They collect power during the day and store it inside somewhere."

"Well those are useful." Shelly started up the walk and climbed the stairs. "Should we ring the bell?"

"Do it." Thomas giggled again.

Everyone stood close behind when Shelly rang the bell. They waited a few minutes but the bell went unanswered.

"I hope Bill didn't disappear too." Thomas worried. "I liked Bill. He'd always give me high-fives every time I came over."

"Who's Bill?" Shelly asked as she rang the bell again.

"He's the doorman." Thomas replied with more cheer.

"Like the butler?" Abby asked.

"No – that's Henry. Bill just gets the door."

Shelly shook her head and rang the bell for the third time and sighed. "Rich people."

"I wish I had a doorman and a butler." Abby mused. "A maid would be nice too, and maybe someone to do my homework for me."

They waited a bit longer but still no response.

"I don't think anyone is coming." Shelly

concluded in disappointment.

"No worries! Lee-dee gave me a key just in case." Thomas dug into his pocket and pulled it out for everyone to see.

"You mean we could have just gone inside?" Shelly asked slightly annoyed.

"I'm sorry." Thomas said as Shelly took his key. "I wanted a high-five."

Percy spoke up with reassurance. "Despite the delay, it was certainly the polite thing to do, Thomas."

"I suppose it was." Shelly agreed as she unlocked the door. "If no one is home, at least we'll be able to see." She opened the door and let everyone enter before her. She then gave Thomas back his key.

"Someone has to be home." Abby deduced. "I mean, rich or not, they are obviously concerned about the planet and wouldn't just leave the lights on all day and night. As she entered the foyer, she clutched her fists together in front of her chest and shook with excitement. "This-is-so-amazing!"

Shelly walked in after her and saw what had sparked such a reaction in her best friend. The floor was marble, with walls fit with white wooden panels, lion claw tables with bushy plants and stone busts of famous people. On the walls were beautiful paintings of far off places and mirrors far larger than any person.

There was a grand staircase that lead up to the higher floor balcony and above that a sparkling glass chandelier.

"Wow." Shelly uttered aloud.

Abby stood next to her. "Wowie-jowie... look at how tall that ceiling is. It's like the gym."

"You could fit an entire warren of rabbits in this room and a little garden as well." Percy admired.

"It's okay." Thomas rolled on his heels and casually skimmed the room. "I'm sure Lee-dee is in her room upstairs—" He spotted someone and pointed to the balcony. "Hi, Lee-dee!"

Shelly and Abby looked to where he was waving and both were struck by a sinking feeling in their stomachs. Slowly and quietly, making her way down the stairs, was a girl in designer jeans, a pink skirted blouse and shoulder length crimped blonde hair. They both knew her too well. It was Lydia Gaines.

Thomas shouted up to her, happy to see his cousin. "Hey, Lee-dee, where is everyone?"

Lydia rudely put her finger up to her lips and harshly shushed him.

Shelly immediately came to his defense. "Don't shush him!"

Lydia shushed her more harshly.

"Listen, Gaines, I didn't bring Thomas here

to be harassed—"

A deep laughter bellowed out into the foyer, echoing from the hallways and somewhere a door slammed.

Lydia stopped in her descent and clutched the railing tightly.

Abby grabbed Shelly's arm in fright. "What was that?

"Lee-dee." Came the haunting voice. "Lee-dee." It spoke again as the pounding of heavy footsteps grew closer by the second. A tinkling came from above, as the chandelier shook with each thump. "Lee-dee. Lee-dee. Lee-dee. Lee-dee. Lee-dee. Lee-dee. Lee-dee. Lee-dee Lee-dee Lee-dee Lee-dee Lee-dee Lee-dee Lee-dee Lee-dee!"

The pounding emerged from the hallway on their right and it neared them like a hungry lion.

Shelly backed away with Abby in tow and Percy leapt into Thomas' arms.

"I think we should go, Shell. Right now!" Abby warned as she retreated.

Shelly didn't question her suggestion. She ran to the door and hastily opened it. She only got it halfway before something heavy struck it and stole the doorknob from her hands. The door slammed shut!

She jumped away just in time to avoid a fountain of spit drop onto the floor from above her. Shelly looked up and screamed from the sight of the creature that clung to the wall like a spider. His body was lean and lanky, as large as an adult, wearing black pajamas and a hideous smile that extended from ear to ear. A long and bumpy tongue lulled out of his mouth that oozed with saliva. He had eight eyes which glowed a fiery red.

As he spoke, he revealed a row of serrated teeth. "Hello, ssssnack." His jaw dislocated, allowing his mouth to open wide enough to swallow Shelly whole.

Just then a bust of Beethoven caught the creature in the chest followed by a well-timed, "Stop!" that pinned him to the wall.

The monster released an ear-piercing shriek as he pushed wildly against the stone head. When he couldn't budge it, he started to scratch at its face and bit the top of the head. As he chewed, his skin took on the same appearance as the stone.

Shelly was paralyzed with fear until she heard Lydia scream, "Run you idiots!"

Both Shelly and Abby raced for the stairs. They both grabbed one of Thomas' arms, and then frantically carried him to the first step and then pushed him forward up the stairs.

Percy navigated the stairs with incredible speed and hopped next to Lydia where he took out his sword and aimed it at the

creature. "Quickly, Thomas!"

"Lee-dee!" The beast taunted between bites; its appearance like that of a statue. "You're fat and nobody loves you. So fat and juicy! No one will miss you."

As they neared the top landing, Lydia grabbed Thomas and ran down an adjacent hallway filled with portraits and several doors.

Percy waved his sword. "You two go ahead. I'll fend off this wretched cur."

Shelly then grabbed him, lifted him off the ground and sped after Lydia and Thomas. "Another time!" Shelly expelled.

The ground shook as something heavy fell to the floor. The creature's voice changed to something deeper and gravel-lier. "I'm going to eat you all!"

His threat echoed through the house.

Lydia burst into her room and ushered everyone inside. Once they cleared the threshold, Lydia closed and locked her door. She rushed behind her dresser and struggled to push it to barricade the door.

"Don't just stand there, stupid, help me!" The blonde yelled at them.

Without further direction, both Shelly and Abby rushed to her aid and they pushed against the dresser with all their strength. It moved quickly into place, and just in time, for as soon as it was put into place, the creature slammed into the door.

As Lydia and Shelly braced against the dresser, Abby ran to other pieces of furniture and levitated them off the floor. With little effort, she pushed it over to meet with the dresser and then commanded them to "Stop", freezing them in place to build up the barricade.

The doorknob twisted and when it couldn't get in, the monster violently banged on the door a couple times before giving up. After what seemed like forever without further noise, everyone released a breath that they had unknowingly held the entire time.

Chapter 8

"What WAS that?!" Abby yelled as quietly as she could. She backed up with Thomas near the bed and stood next to him.

"He knows we're in here, dummy. You don't need to whisper." Lydia replied harshly. "Thanks, by-the-way, for bringing my little cousin into danger."

"Don't be mean to her." Shelly barked back. "How could we possibly know you keep monsters in your house?"

"He's not a monster, he's my brother." Lydia glared at her.

"That's Alex?" Thomas asked while hugging Percy.

"Why is your brother trying to hurt us?" Shelly demanded as she stared down the blonde.

Lydia tilted her head with a devious smile. "Your eyes are going to pop out of your head looking like that."

Shelly scoffed but refused to back down.

"What's wrong with Alex, Lee-dee?" Thomas begged.

Lydia gave up her staring contest. "How should I know?" She waved off his question and placed her hand on her hip. "We don't hang out."

"When did he start acting strange?" Abby

asked with caution.

"He's always acted strange." Was her snap response.

Shelly jumped sharply into the conversation. "She means climbing the walls strange. Stop trying to win a popularity contest and answer her question."

She puckered her lips. "Sweetie, I don't try. I do."

"You know what? – Fine! We don't have to be here. We came for Thomas because we thought he would be better off with his family. I was totally wrong. You're obviously too wrapped up in yourself. Abby, do you think you can make a staircase out of books or something to help us out a window?"

Percy hopped to the floor. "Ladies, if I may interject."

Lydia pointed to the rabbit. "Are you doing this, Thomas?"

Thomas raised his hands in celebration. "I have no idea!" He laughed.

Percy cleared his throat. "Lee-dee, I know things are very overwhelming right now and judging from the conversation, you two share some mutual ire. Let's try and put that aside and think what is best for the now. Lady Abby and Lady Shelly came to our rescue when we were beset by a fell dragon."

"It was Snappers." Thomas interrupted

joyously.

"Quite right, Thomas." Percy agreed. "It appears that you are also in a bit of a jam. If we all work together, we may be able to escape the terror that plagues you and then hash out old grievances then. What do you say?"

Lydia brushed the hair from her eyes and then looked over at Thomas for an explanation.

"He came to life this morning. We've been playing games all day." He chuckled.

She drooped her head to her shoulder and sighed. "I suppose." She offered with little confidence. "Alex was sick this morning. All the help was gone and so I was the one who had to baby him. He got a fever. No matter what I did, he only got worse. Later he started mumbling to himself, it was nothing at first and mostly about family things, then he started forgetting things."

"Forgetting?" Thomas asked with a scrunch of his brow.

"Like what?" Abby inquired.

She rolled her head to the other side as if Abby had made it uncomfortable. "He talked about our trip to the Badlands. He kept insisting that I had been selfish and always had to get my way."

"Sounds about right." Shelly interrupted.

"He was talking about when we stopped for ice cream. He was the one who insisted that I beg mom and dad to stop. I don't even like ice cream. I did it for him because if he had asked they wouldn't have stopped."

Shelly's brow wrinkled.

"That's... weird." Abby offered.

"He just got worse. He started accusing me of things. Things I've never done. He started calling me names. I left soon after that. I later found him roaming the halls. When he saw me, he started to change..." Her eyes grew distant, a touch of pain crossed her face and for a moment she was lost in a thought. "Anyway, it wasn't long after that when you all showed up. You know the rest."

"It sounds like there is more to the story." Shelly accused. "Something else happened. How did he change? What do you mean by he changed?"

"He's evil, okay!" Lydia screamed with tearful eyes. "He's down right evil. He isn't Alex anymore."

Despite their history, Shelly felt bad for her. It's her tears – they made her seem more like a person instead of a bully.

Shelly took a step forward, just as Lydia turned away to wipe her eyes with her sleeve. "Please... Lydia, we need to know."

The lone Gaines sniffed to draw all her

vulnerability back inside herself. "Tough." She replied sternly.

"What can you tell us, Lee-dee?" The rabbit asked as his button eyes watched her sympathetically.

She's sharp with her answer. "He becomes what he eats and he's always hungry."

"And he can climb walls." Shelly added.

Lydia rolled her eyes. "He ate a spider."

"Gross!" Abby protested.

"So what are we going to do?" Thomas asked the room.

"I say we fight it." Shelly exclaimed as she tightened her fist. "We can't have something like this running around town. What happens if it eats someone?"

"The jock is right." Lydia reassured with a touch of resentment. "We have to stop him somehow."

"I'm glad to see that the two of you agree on something. How do you intend to stop him?" Percy asked.

"Abby? How long can you make Alex float?" Shelly asked.

She shook her head. "Not at all. I'm afraid it doesn't work on people. I've tried."

"So that's why you threw the bust." Lydia mentioned.

Shelly felt as if Lydia was going to say something insulting but was surprised when nothing followed.

"Well, that idea's out." Shelly followed up in disappointment.

"There's always what happened with the car." Abby pointed out in a mousy voice.

Lydia beamed at Shelly with suspicion. "What happened to the car, Whinny?"

Shelly looked at her hoop. "I don't think that's such a good idea. I could miss."

"I told you my secrets!" Lydia argued. "So spit it out!"

"It's a little hard to explain, exactly." Shelly advised out of caution.

"Then show us, unless of course you're too scared."

"There's too many people in here. I could hit someone." Shelly explained with irritation.

Lydia pointed at her hoop. "Then don't suck."

"Fine." Shelly relented in slight anger.

She moved to the center of the large bedroom. With a quick shift of her shoulder she brought the hoop down to her hands and she hastened the ring into figure eights. She engaged quickly, fueled by her desire to show Lydia up, and in mere seconds the hoop lit up. The ring heated the air around her and the room grew hot. Shelly stopped it and the light slowly diminished.

"It can cut through steel when it gets bright

enough." Shelly boasted.

Lydia stood unimpressed but calculated something in her head.

"So, what?" Shelly demanded with impatience.

"I'm sorry, was that a question?" She beamed a fake smile.

Shelly returned it. "So... Thomas can bring stuffed animals to life and Abby can make objects float and stop mid-air. What can you do?"

Lydia displayed her right hand and instantly bathed the room with a blinding light. It lasted only a moment before it drew back into her palm.

"I can fix you if you're broken."

Chapter 9

Shelly poked her head out of the door and searched the hallway beyond the dents and crushed doorknob.

See anything?" Abby whispered from behind her.

"Nope. All clear." Shelly announced.

Someone pushed from behind and Shelly tripped out into the hall. Shelly almost face-planted. Once she recovered, she tagged the culprit with her eyes.

"I hope your throw is better than your balance, Whinny." Lydia commented as she straightened her spine to appear taller.

Thomas quietly followed her with Percy keeping close to his legs.

"Be careful, Thomas. Stay close to Lee-dee and me." The rabbit twitched his nose and strained his ears.

"Are you sure this is the right thing to do?" Thomas begged. "It's Alex, right? We're family, aren't we? Maybe we can fix him somehow."

His cousin abandoned her taunting and leaned down to look him in the eyes. "No matter what happens, you have to remember that that thing is not Alex. It is a monster. It may look like him and at times it may sound like him, but it's not him, Thomas. It will kill any of us. It will eat us – bones and all. We have to do this, Thomas."

She glared back at her competition from beneath her blonde locks. "Don't hesitate or you'll kill us, got it?"

"Yeah – I got it."

"This is a bit too much." Abby jittered from the doorway. "I can do what you asked, earlier. I can make stairs from books like you said, we don't have to do anything. I could seal the house up with cars or something and we could all go home."

"Until it eats its way out. Can you sleep with your eyes open?" Lydia asked. When no answer came from the redhead she straightened back up and sighed. "I didn't think so."

"As much as I hate to say this, Lydia is right." Shelly added with cold determination. "If he's a monster, then we have to do our best to get rid of him."

"If you ladies don't mind me asking," the stuffed rabbit interrupted as he drew his toy sword, "What's our plan of attack?"

Shelly took in a deep breath and gripped her hoop tightly. "Not get eaten."

As a group, they started down the hall with Shelly in the lead. They moved as quietly as possible, keeping their ears attuned to the slightest noise. Lydia kept a few paces behind Shelly to give her room in case she needed to use her hoop, while Thomas, Percy and Abby kept farther back.

Without warning, the lights flickered and then the house was drowned in darkness.

"What happened? Why are the lights off?" Abby whispered in fright.

"Lee-dee?" Thomas begged a little louder.

"Shush—" Lydia snapped back. "He'll hear us."

The hallway lit back up as the blonde ignited her hand in a soft glow.

Now able to see, Abby pulled out her flashlight and turned it on. Quickly, she shined it outside Lydia's light radius, searching every dark corner she could imagine where a monster could hide. Her hand trembled.

"Do you think it was Alex?" Shelly asked as she tried to look ahead.

"Duh." Lydia taunted.

Shelly narrowed her eyes. "I really don't like you."

"Thank you, Captain Obvious." She responded with sass.

The house transformed as soon as the light had gone. Where once it was warm and inviting, it was replaced by something frightening and sinister. The house belonged to him now and they were his prey.

"I'm scared, Percy." Thomas whispered as he clung to Abby's arm.

"There's nothing wrong with being afraid." The rabbit counseled. "Everyone is afraid sometimes."

Lydia remarked, "I'm afraid of Shelly missing and all of us being eaten alive."

"Do you want to throw it?" Shelly forced in a heavy whisper.

"I can't make burning death hoops or I would." She replied.

They reached the stairs and you noticed how the floor below was thick in darkness.

"Abby, can you shine your light below us?" Shelly asked as she pointed over the railing.

"Is he down there?" She asked in fright.

"That's why she's asking you to shine the light, stupid, so we can find out."

"Can you just shut up for a minute?" Shelly demanded.

Abby inched over to her, fearful that something would grab her and pull her into the void below. She swallowed hard and did her best to be courageous enough, at least, to point the light where Shelly had directed. She canvassed the floor and then darted the light over the door, to a table and then to an adjoining hall. With each pass, her heart jumped, due to fearing it would reveal something horrifying.

"Come on." Shelly motioned as she took the first step down the stairs.

She took her hula hoop off her shoulder and held it readily in front of her.

Little by little, one after another, they descended the staircase. Each step tied knots in their stomachs. When Shelly reached the last step, she carefully placed her foot on the ground as if worried that it would fall out from under her.

Lydia raised her hand higher to try and extend the light of her power farther into the room without exerting herself.

The bust Abby had thrown earlier was now nothing more than a few bits and pieces. The wall above the door revealed heavy scratches deep in the wood.

When they reached the center floor, they stopped with panic as they heard a sound shifting in the walls around them, like the writhing of worms in a bait jar. Abby shined her light in every which direction, desperate to find the source.

They heard a slithering noise, a light tapping and then it all grew quiet.

Abby asked, "Do you think it's gone?"

Before anyone could respond, something snagged around her ankle and Abby was dragged to the floor. She dropped her flashlight and it went spinning across the room as she screamed. Before anyone knew what had happened, Abby was pulled through a pair of doors and into the darkness of a distant corridor.

"Abby!" Shelly yelled as she ran after her.

Her best friend continued to scream as she was drawn farther and farther into the house.

Abby wildly grabbed onto whatever she could, but she couldn't hold onto it long enough as the objects all spun weightlessly away from her.

Shelly sped into the hallway, her shoes lit up by the light of her own power. The place was filled with floating tables, vases and the carpet also twisted about in the surreal. Shelly did her best to dodge them while keeping her speed.

"Abby!" Shelly shouted with hope her words would draw her back from the darkness.

Lydia couldn't keep up. Before she would run neck to neck with her. It was too easy to beat her this time, Shelly's powers made sure of that. She made several strides only in a manner of seconds. Shelly blazed past a second pair of double doors and into a grand dining room. By the light of her own feet, she was able to make out the contents.

Electrical wires hung from the ceiling and were attached, somehow, to Alex, which suspended him above the dinner table. He held Abby upside down by the foot, with several wires wrapped around her ankle that slowly drew her towards his gaping mouth.

Shelly didn't think, didn't hesitate as she masterfully spun her hoop around her body. It was the fastest that she had ever performed. Once the ring grew hot, she tossed it at the abomination with a well-aimed throw.

Lydia entered the room as soon as the hoop whizzed through the air and severed the wires gripping Abby's feet. The red-head dropped like a sack of laundry onto the table below her. The hoop then embedded itself into the back wall with a shower of sparks. Shelly had aimed for his torso. She couldn't believe it... she missed.

The monster writhed in pain and turned his gaze against her. His eyes burned with hellish rage. His face was coiled wire. He opened his mouth and he released a growl. His teeth sparked with electricity from the exposed copper that was fed by the heavy battery that made up his abdomen.

Thomas stopped at the door with Percy and released a scream before he could cover his mouth.

"Stay here!" Lydia yelled back as she ran up alongside Shelly.

Abby took a little time to recover as the fall had stolen some of her breath. She

managed to roll off the table and hide beneath it.

The coiled creature lowered itself from the ceiling. The wires wiggled about his body like a den of angered vipers.

"You missed!" Lydia accused Shelly.

"Not entirely!" Shelly argued as braced herself for what came next.

Alex leapt at them.

Shelly tried to dodge out of the way, but Alex was too quick. With one swipe of his arm, he battered her hard enough to send her flying across the room and into a china cabinet.

"Wynn!" Lydia shouted after her in a moment of care.

When Shelly hit, she heard a crack and her body welled with pain. She cried out in agony.

Like Abby before her, Lydia was snatched up by several tendrils of wire that wrapped about her waist. The abomination craned his neck like an extension cord and drew open its mouth.

"You're fat Lydia. Fat and tasty. You're a terrible person. No one loves you, except my stomach."

The mouth opened, expanded and stretched to fit around her head. His teeth sparked violently with the anticipation of the meal.

"No! Alex, stop!" Lydia threw both her

hands in front of her and the entire room was blinded by a white light.

The monster cringed beneath the intrusion, which momentarily stalled him from chomping down on her head. It was long enough for Lydia to feel soft paws climb up her leg, onto her shoulders and then atop her head.

When her vision returned, a rabbit leveled its toy sword at the creature's head.

"Leave Lee-Dee alone, you fiend!" Percy cried as he stabbed the demon right in his eye.

Alex let go of Lydia as he recoiled in pain. The monster frantically grabbed at his wound, where instead of an eye, only sparks of electricity danced.

The monster's pain spurred enough bravery from Abby to escape from beneath the table and rush over to Shelly's hoop and she tried to pry it free. Lydia did not squander her opportunity either, as she grabbed Percy and rushed over to Shelly's aid.

Shelly held her arm close to her chest as she propped herself against the wooden cabinet. "It hurts." She managed while biting back tears. "I think it's broken."

"Stop being a baby." Lydia placed both her hands on Shelly's arm and channeled her light into her. Shelly's eyes and mouth lit up like a jack-o-lantern. In an instant, the pain was gone and Shelly could move her arm again.

Shelly looked to her limb, moved her hand as if it were for the first time, and then gazed back at Lydia.

"Thanks Ly—" Was all that Shelly could get out before Lydia yanked her upwards.

"Get up pansy!" Lydia barked as she pushed Shelly towards where Abby was desperately trying to free the hoop from the wall.

Percy hastily made his way back to Thomas and yelled to them, "Hurry girls! You mustn't remain in one place. Make him work for his dinner."

Alex uncovered his eye, now free from the wincing and turned his remaining eye against the rabbit and Thomas. He slithered his way across the floor, and then slung himself like an orangutan to close the distance between them.

"Thomas!" Lydia screamed out.

"You distract Alex, I'll get my hoop." Shelly commanded as she sped to Abby's side.

"Right—" Lydia called back. "Hey outlet breath!" She yelled at her freakish brother. "I'm right here!"

Alex stopped and extended his head behind his body and glared at her with a blood blazing eye.

"Mom and Dad said I was their favorite!"

Lydia taunted him.

"You're going to die, Lee-dee!" Alex howled as his body reoriented itself so he could chase her. Abby and Shelly both put their foot up against the wall and gave the hoop one sharp tug – jimmying it loose. Abby then darted out of her way.

Shelly twirled and spun as quickly as she could, letting the hoop grow hotter and brighter with every second.

Lydia backed up against the wall. "Do it, Shelly!"

Alex vaulted himself up onto the dining table then jumped down onto the ground.

"You hungry!?" Shelly bellowed. "Then eat this!"

She flung the hoop across the distance between them and it cleaved straight through his abdomen, splitting the battery in two and throwing acid out onto the floor. The brute's torso separated from his legs and both parts fell into a mess on the floor.

The hoop floated harmlessly in the air as Abby commanded it to stop to prevent it from harming anything. Without momentum, the heat slowly dissipated and the hula-hoop was harmless once more.

Chapter 10

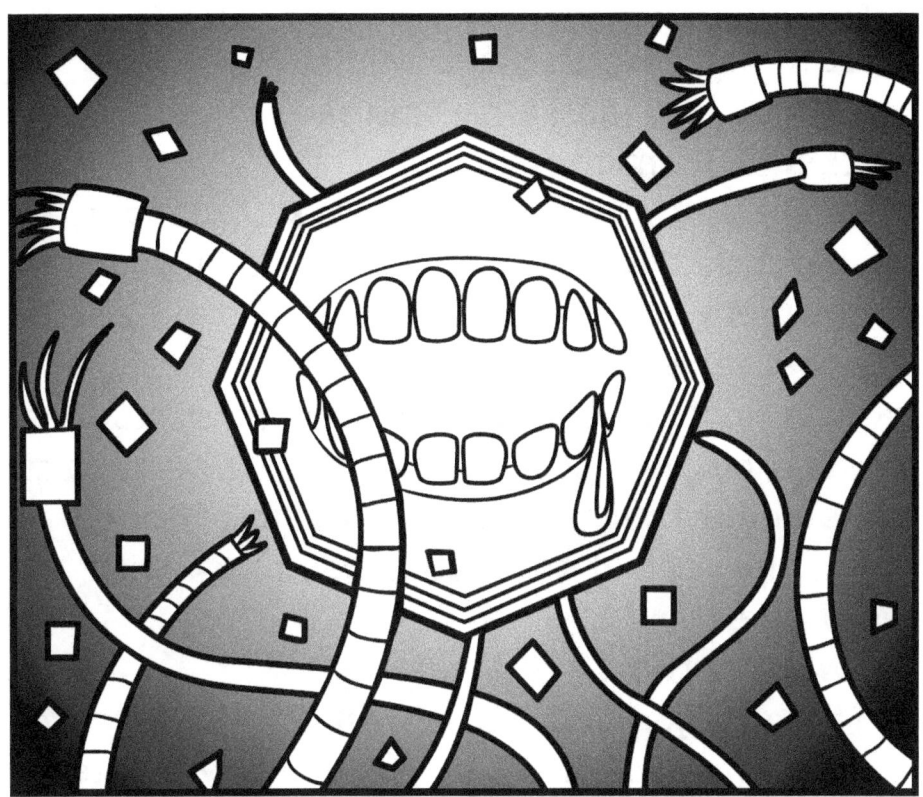

The creature fell apart and its wires slowly curled up into themselves like a spider. Lydia lifted her hand to bring light to the room.

"Is he," Abby asked with a quiver to her voice. "...dead?"

Alex's body slowly peeled away like a piñata. Tiny pieces of confetti drifted up into the air before burning up into tiny tufts of ash. Everyone was quiet as they watched. When all the wires fully disintegrated, the only thing left behind was a small shimmering object that hovered like a wisp in the air.

Lydia slowly inched towards it to gain a better look. It wasn't until she was halfway between Shelly and the glow that she realized what it was. While Lydia was hesitant, and though against all sense and reason, she plucked it from the air.

Shelly and Abby, seeing a lack of danger, approached Lydia to examine it. It fit snuggly in the palm of her hand. It was a round patch, like the one's the varsity kids wore on their jackets. Instead of mascots and cheer slogans, it was a portrait of a pair of teeth with reddish gums and a touch of drool hanging off one side. The rest of the patch was black with a red border.

"What is that?" Thomas asked.

The girls jumped out of fright.

"Oh, Thomas! It's just you." Abby inhaled to slow her heart.

Somehow, he had made it from the entryway to the back of the room without anyone noticing.

"A patch, I think." Shelly informed him.

"Wow – really? Great assessment there, Whinny. No wonder you get so many 'A's in class."

Shelly narrowed her eyes with resentment. "You don't know when to quit, do you?"

"If it came from that terrible monster, then we shouldn't have anything to do with it."

Abby mentioned.

Lydia closed her hands around it harshly. "It came from Alex, so it belongs to me."

Shelly grabbed Lydia's wrist. "Don't be insane. This is probably what made him go nuts to begin with."

Lydia pulled her hand free. "This is my house, Shelly Wynn. That was my brother! I will do whatever I want." She glared at her with undoubting conviction.

"Fine! See what I care." Shelly waved her off.

Shelly decided to give up before she got into a fight. She walked away and snatched up her hoop.

Lydia gave her an icy stare before glancing down at her cousin. Thomas hugged Percy as tightly as he could, looking a bit overwhelmed from tonight and too nervous to say anything more.

The blonde took in a breath. "I think it's time to call it a night, Thomas."

"Yes – too much excitement for one night." Percy agreed.

"You can stay with me, if you'd like. Abby is also staying over." Shelly offered.

"Don't be ridiculous." Lydia stepped in. "Thomas is staying with me."

"Here? Are you insane? He'll have nightmares."

"Not here, moron. At his house."

Shelly sighed with frustration. "Whatever."

"I'll need to get my things and then I'll be ready. Thomas and Percy will accompany me to my bedroom and you two will remain in the foyer. Oh – that's the room where the front door is."

"I know what a foyer is."

"Perfect, then after you." Lydia insisted.

Abby stood nearest the door, one hand on the knob and the other on her flashlight combing the house in case another monster would appear. She was ready to leave.

Shelly twirled her hoop between her wrists and then up and down her arms, while trying to keep the light it emitted from becoming too bright. She occasionally cast an impatient look up the stairs for any sign of Thomas, Percy or Lydia.

"I really hate her." Shelly thought aloud. "She's making us wait on purpose."

"Her brother just turned into a monster and you cut him in half. You may want to give her a little slack – at least for today." Abby voiced with caution. She didn't want to pick a fight, especially not over someone like Lydia Gaines.

"She's like this all the time! You'd think she'd be different considering the circumstances, but nope – same old Lydia." Shelly continued to hoop, racing it up and down her torso. She tried to judge the speed versus the light it gave off.

"Maybe it's a defense mechanism? You know, like how she deals with stress or other bad stuff."

Shelly stopped her hoop in mid-spin. "She's been dealing since kindergarten. People are her friends as long as she gets her way. We both know how she is."

Abby shrugged. In the dark, Shelly didn't even notice.

"I'm not saying that we need to be her friends, I'm just saying that for tonight we should let it be. Try to ignore her no matter how nasty she is."

"I guess so." Shelly sighed. "I probably shouldn't let her get under my skin but she's just so good at it."

A series of loud clanks, like a rapid pile driver banged into the ground. The floor shook with each strike.

"Do you hear that?" Shelly asked her friend.

Abby took her hand off the knob. "I can feel it. The door is shaking." She stepped away from the threshold and moved with Shelly towards the center floor. "It's getting closer."

Clank Ca-Clank-Ca-Clank, Clank.

The sound came closer like some gigantic creature with several legs, breaking up the street with each step and sending vibrations into their feet. Shelly felt it in her chest and it caused her heart to skip a beat. Whatever it was, it was nearing by the moment.

A light came from the balcony. "What are you idiots doing?" Lydia demanded. Thomas and Percy weren't far behind her.

Shelly shushed her with a single finger to her mouth.

Lydia inhaled for a fight. "Don't shush me in my own house!"

The ground shook violently. A loud metallic creature swept across the second story windows facing the street.

"There's something outside!" Abby shrieked as she took Shelly by the hand and raced up the stairs.

A hiss erupted from the front of the house and the windows instantly fogged up like the breath of some behemoth.

"Oh-God-oh-God-oh-God-oh-God." Abby prayed as the two of them scrambled up the stairs. "Not again!"

Lydia released the light from her hand and ducked beneath the railing. She motioned for Thomas and Percy to hide back in the hallway.

A loud moan pushed through the cracks in

the home and then everything went quiet. Shelly and Abby slid down onto the floor and joined Lydia at her hiding place. Everyone held their breath.

A gigantic eye opened at one of the windows and threw down a spotlight onto the center floor. The light cascaded, as Abby had previously done with the flashlight, in every corner and cranny as if searching for something or someone. Abby gave off a whimper that she tried to stifle but it was too late. The noise was enough to shift the spotlight to their location.

The light burned their eyes as they tried to shield it away. The brightness remained on them for a few seconds before shutting off, leaving them in complete darkness. The metal then screeched as it lowered towards the front door and then there was the groaning of wood.

A small light, as if someone had turned on a hallway lamp, filtered in from beneath the front door. Just as they feared the worse, a few envelopes were tossed through the mail slot.

Without a blink or word goodbye, the light disappeared and the metallic sounds returned. With several clanks and whirring, the object rose once more into the air and moved away. It could be heard as it continued farther down the street.

As soon as the rumblings had dissipated, Thomas peeked his head from the hallway. "Is it gone?" He begged while he trembled.

"It appears that way." Lydia replied as she rose to her feet.

"What was that thing?" Abby asked as she slowly inspired herself to standing.

"I don't know, McMullen. Why don't you go run after it and find out."

Abby apparently had enough of tonight and almost forgot what she had encouraged Shelly of earlier. "It was a rhetorical question." She huffed.

"There's no such thing as a rhetorical question. If you don't want an answer, don't ask for one." The blonde-haired teen huffed as she lit her hand.

Shelly gave her a nasty glare.

Lydia pointed at the door and returned Shelly's look. "Make yourself useful and see what arrived."

"And then, Abby and I are leaving." Shelly announced as she stomped her way down the stairs in hopes of annoying Lydia.

Abby followed in a lighter step, as well as Thomas and Percy. Lydia was not far behind.

Abby turned on her flashlight and aimed it in the direction of the mailbox to see what filtered through. There were four purple envelopes, each with their names embossed on the front in fancy gold lettering.

Shelly picked them up and handed them out respectively. "Sorry, Percy." Shelly said as she passed him over. "There isn't one here for you."

"Quite all right, Lady Shelly. I doubt the post even knows I've taken residence."

Everyone tore into their envelope at the same time and withdrew a small invitation. Abby read hers aloud, "Parentless? Alone? The world is harsh without someone to tuck you in at night. Not to fret. The SOK Market is open for your every need. We cordially invite you, tomorrow morning at 10, sharp. Don't be late. 15 ½ Ash Street."

Shelly looked up from reading. "Do you think they'll know where our parents are?"

"It says, 'open for your every need', so they have to know something." Abby replied.

"More than you'd think." Lydia added, her nose buried in her invitation. She pulled out a small business card that was attached to her invitation and read it aloud. "Congratulations on your recent acquisition. You are the first owner of a SOK patch. Bring it with you for additional services, free of charge."

Thomas placed his finger near his mouth. "How did they know about that?" He asked with confusion.

Lydia was about to say something but Shelly purposefully interrupted her. "Whatever is going on with our parents, with Alex, the lights, all of it may be answered at this SOK Market. We should all meet there tomorrow. Right now, it's getting too late for anything else."

"Am I assuming right that there won't be school tomorrow either?" Asked Abby.

"Great deduction Watson, like you'd go if there was. As far as I'm concerned, tomorrow is a mental health day." Lydia grabbed Thomas' hand. "Come on, Thomas, it's time to go."

Both Thomas and Percy nodded and the tiny rabbit waved to both Abby and Shelly. "Farewell dear Ladies, thank you again for your earlier assistance." Percy bowed.

Lydia opened the front door and held it open so that everyone would get out.

Abby hurried down the dark steps and scanned the outside with her flashlight. There were now two large holes in the sidewalk and several others in the yard, but their bicycles were unharmed. She kicked up the stand and looked back at Shelly who had just shouldered her hoop and followed after.

Shelly paused as she watched Thomas retrieve his and Lydia's backpack. She was reluctant to leave the boy in her hands. She had to keep telling herself that they were cousins and that she'll take care of him. If only she could believe it.

Lydia caught her staring and bugged her eyes out momentarily to show her irritation. It was that moment, Shelly was reminded it was better for everyone to leave well enough alone – which meant getting as far away from Lydia as possible.

"See you later, Thomas. Take care, Percy." Shelly called behind her as she and Abby started pedaling back towards the street.

"Bye!" Abby yelled back.

Abby led the way with her flashlight.

Together, they rode off quickly into the night.

Chapter 11

The two girls dragged themselves into Shelly's house and immediately made their way to the kitchen.

"I'm starving!" Abby declared with a groan as she plopped herself on a stool near the island counter.

Shelly opened the refrigerator and noted the lack of cold and the silence of its motor. Since the power was off the microwave, the oven and the freezer couldn't be used either. She hadn't realized it before, but the kitchen was kind of creepy without the low buzz of appliances. Her mother always told her that if she ever bought a stove to get a gas one, just in case something like this happened. At least they could still cook something.

She grabbed a juice for herself and she slid one across the counter for Abby.

"The refrigerator isn't on. Last time this happened, we had to eat as much as we could because by tomorrow it'll all go bad."

"I'll eat anything!" Abby said as she twisted the top off the bottle and took a long drink. She had finished nearly half of it before coming up for air. "What do you have?"

Shelly shined the light inside the refrigerator. "We have steaks, eggs, bacon, salad... some leftover meatloaf."

"Sounds good." Abby nodded. "Hey, what about ice cream? Do you have any?"

"Um..." Shelly checked the bottom freezer. "We do have ice cream."

"We should probably eat that too... you know, before it goes bad." Abby encouraged with a sly smile.

Shelly poked the container. "It's a little squishy."

"Then we shouldn't wait. We should eat it right now."

"I like how you think." Shelly pulled out two tubs of ice cream – French vanilla and Rocky Road and showed them to her friend. "Which one do you want?"

"Yes!" She joked.

Shelly laughed. "All right then. French rocky road vanilla it is." She paused. "We should probably save the flashlights because I don't know if we have any batteries. Can you grab the candles out of the living room and bring them here?"

"Good idea." Abby complimented as she pried herself off her seat and took the light with her into the living room.

Shelly fumbled around in the utensil drawer, going mostly off feel and memory before she found a couple of spoons. She placed them on the counter and then shuffled around in the upper cabinets and found some bowls.

Abby returned with two of the larger candles and put them on the counter.

"There should be a lighter in the drawer near the dishwasher on the right-hand side." Shelly instructed as she spooned a few scoops into each of their own respective bowls.

Abby was able to locate what she needed and lit the candles. As soon as the wicks grew bright enough, Abby shut off her light and set the flashlight aside.

"I can't remember the last time my parents allowed me to use candles." Abby mused.

Shelly offered Abby the ice cream, who then immediately snatched up the dish and shoved a spoonful into her mouth.

"Can you imagine?" Abby said with a mouth full. "How much ice cream is going bad? All over town. It must be a lot."

"Not to mention all the ice cream in the grocery stores."

Abby suspended her spoon of ice cream in front of her mouth to swallow. "I think they have backup generators or something. Probably won't last forever though." She took another bite.

"Maybe we should go grocery shopping after the whole SOK market thing?" Shelly pointed with her spoon.

"How are we going to pay for it?"

"My mom has a credit card in her dresser for emergencies."

"But the power's out, so the swipe machines won't work. Not to mention there's no one going to be at the counter to take our money."

Shelly thought for a moment. "We could always leave an IOU or something. My mom has store credit there anyway."

"Smart thinking!" Abby complimented with enthusiasm. "Then they can always charge your mom when everyone gets back. We'll need to get things that don't refrigerate, especially if we don't have power." Abby sighed and then placed her spoon on the table.

"What's the matter?"

"What if the power never comes back on? I mean... if our parents don't come back, then who will get it working again?"

"Abby," Shelly tried to be as sympathetic as possible. "Our parents are coming back. They'll do whatever it takes to get back home."

"You think so?" Abby asked with some hope in her voice.

"Of course, I do. Wouldn't you do anything to get back home if you suddenly disappeared?"

"I suppose you're right." The redhead

nodded. "They can't be gone forever."

Shelly ate a spoonful of French vanilla and waited a few moments. Despite the comfort food, she relived the moment she sliced that monster in half. She worried.

"Abby? Do you think I did the right thing?"

"With what, exactly?" She asked as she tilted her head.

She bit her lip. "What I did to Alex."

"Shell, if I could make hoops the way you do I would have cut it down too, or at least tried." She paused. "No, I'm lying. I would have ran. But it was a monster, Shell. It tried to eat me and Lydia. It wasn't good. As far as I'm concerned, everyone is alive because of you. Who knows what that thing would have done?"

Shelly sighed. "Thanks Abby. I've been thinking about it and how it was her brother and all. I don't know... maybe it's because he was a kid once or maybe it's because Lydia told me to do it. I'm not sure."

Abby reached out and touched her friend's hand. "It was nothing more than a monster. It's not going to hurt anyone else. That's what is important." She took her hand back and ate some more ice cream. "Besides, Lydia doesn't seem that upset about it."

"I think her level of meanness overrides her level of compassion." Shelly pointed out as she set her bowl down. "I'm done with this." In reference to the ice cream.

"Steaks?" Abby asked with a raised brow.

Shelly nodded her head with agreement and took out a pan along with a few spices like her father had taught her.

"Do you miss your parents at all, Abby? I mean like, really miss them?"

Abby took a mental inventory and then shook her head. "Not really. I worry about them though."

"Do you feel sad that they are gone?"

Abby shook her head again. "Nope."

"Me either." Shelly slapped the steak into the pan. "Isn't that weird to say that?" She turned up the gas burners. She reached backwards. "Can you hand me a candle?"

"Like this?" Abby giggled as she caused one of the candles to float and she gently nudged it towards Shelly.

Shelly shook her head and picked it up out of the air, giving a small chuckle. "I like this ability of yours. It's a lot of fun."

"Hey!?" Abby exclaimed. "Tomorrow, if things aren't back to normal, I want to see if I can make a car float." Abby declared with excitement.

Shelly laughed as she lit the burner with the candle. "Why would you want to do that?" She was careful not to spill any of the

wax.

"I dunno – to see if I can? Plus, weren't we supposed to have flying cars by now?"

Shelly flipped the steak and shrugged her shoulders with a smile. "I don't know, did you read that somewhere?"

"Nope, I saw it in a movie."

"You could always try lifting Mr. Martin's car in the alley. It's already damaged."

"And if I break it some more, I'll just blame you." She laughed.

"Some friend you are!" Shelly accused jokingly.

"Hey – I came with you to check on everyone, didn't I?"

Shelly put the handle of the spatula to her chin. "Hmm..." She teased. "You most certainly did. Thank you for coming out with me. I don't think I would have left Lydia's house in one piece if it wasn't for you."

"Well – I didn't want to be alone in the dark. I'd take Lydia's abuse over that any day."

Shelly took the steaks out of the pan and served them up on a plate. She took out a knife and fork for each of them and then poured them both a glass of water.

"There! Bon appetit."

They ate and then wound down the rest of their night before heading to bed. Despite having taken a nap, the encounter with Lydia's brother had taken a lot out of Shelly. She was exhausted.

Abby and Shelly changed into their pajamas and both shared Shelly's bed. With the covers up tight, Abby stared out into the darkness of the room and felt that familiar gnaw of fear.

"Shell?"

"Hm?" Shelly expelled as she relaxed into her mattress.

"Do you think it's bad that I'm still scared of the dark?"

Shelly inhaled one last time before falling into shallow breaths. "I think a lot of people are scared of the dark."

"But you're not scared."

"I'm scared of other things."

"Like what?"

"Failing... for one. Not being in control. You know... weird things."

"That's not that weird." She sighed. "Goodnight, Sun."

Shelly yawned. "Goodnight, Moon."

They both closed their eyes and slowly drifted into sleep.

Chapter 12

Shelly heard a familiar voice trying to stir her from her slumber. "Shelly-bean. Hey there, Shelly-bean. It's time to wake up."

A hand brushed the hair from her face as her eyes slowly blinked open.

There was a figure sitting on the side of her bed, fuzzy at first, but then she recognized him.

"Dad?"

It was daylight, sometime in the early morning, as the light filtered through her blinds and illuminated him in a peculiar way.

"Dad!" She quickly rose from her pillow and wrapped her arms around him. Her cheek brushed up against his coarse bristles but she was too happy to care.

"That's right, beanie." He hugged her back.

"When did you get back?" She asked as she relaxed her hug and settled back in the bed.

"Just this morning."

"Is mom home too?"

"Of course, she is, silly. What a strange question. Now, it's time to get up – you're going to be late."

Shelly scrunched her eyebrows. "Late for what, dad?"

Her eyes opened and she found that her head had never left her pillow. There was no sign of her father or that anyone had been in her room except the still sleeping Abigail McMullen.

Late? She remembered that the invitation had said 10 a.m. – Don't be late. She didn't have a watch and all the clocks in the house were digital. Maybe her mother's cellphone still had power. Shelly leapt out of bed, startled to see that the day had already began without her and praying that it was still early morning.

Her mom's cell was dangerously low but still it revealed the time – 9:20 a.m.

"Oh-no!" She dropped the phone and raced through her room in pursuit of clothes. "Abby! Get up! We're going to be late!"

"Huh?" The now fluffy haired girl rose from her sheets and rubbed her eyes to separate herself from a dream.

"It's almost 9:30 – the invitation said ten – We've got to go!"

The bed-bound teen blinked her eyes wide, took a few moments to realize what was said to her and then sprung out of bed to join Shelly in her own clothing hunt.

Both hastily changed, then stumbled down the stairs while brushing their hair, and quickly put on their shoes and rushed outside – shutting the door behind them.

They took their bikes down the empty

street and turned down Rhine, past the corner store and up the hill where the church stood.

"What's the address again?" Abby asked as she struggled to keep up.

Shelly's ability to infuse her hoop energized her pedaling, with the gears of her bike glowing with the same white light. She had a tough time restricting her speed so not to leave Abby behind.

"15 ½ Ash Street. I know how to get there. I took piano lessons from Ms. Edgewater. She lives on the same street."

"I didn't know you played piano." Abby shouted.

"I don't. I was terrible at it." Shelly called back as she turned onto the right road.

Shelly knew that they were in the right place the moment she spied Lydia, Thomas and then Percy. Even as far away as she was, she could envision a sneer on the girl's face while Thomas waved and laughed.

As they both neared, Shelly's eyes fixated on the colossal thing that had mysteriously plopped itself between two houses. The mere sight of it caused her to slam on her handle breaks.

It was a ghastly old house with paint peeling from the windows, missing siding and loose shingles that all were a dreary grey color. It had multiple stories and a widow's

walk at the very top. All her favorite TV shows had warned her that bad things happened in these types of houses. What made everything all the more chilling was the giant holes, the size of her hands, that lead like a pair of tracks from beneath the house, across the lawn and down the street; the very same tracks that she noticed outside Lydia's house.

Shelly knew this house wasn't here when she took lessons years before. It was almost as if the house had picked itself up, walked and then sat down.

As the two of them placed their bicycles on the ground, the neon sign hanging over the porch flickered on reading, "SOK Market".

"Are we sure we want to go in?" Abby asked as she cringed.

"If you're too scared, there's a daycare down the street. I'm sure someone there could babysit you." Lydia taunted with a tilt of her head.

"There's nothing to be scared of." Thomas giggled. "Monsters don't come out during the day, right Percy?"

"Quite right," The stuffed rabbit advised. "Why, the sheer sight of us would send any villains running for the hills."

"I'm not scared." Abby stated in self-defense. Then she mumbled, "Just cautious."

"I'm not waiting for you losers anymore. Come on, Thomas. Try to stay close. It's probably dirty inside."

Lydia bravely climbed the steps of the rickety porch. She didn't bother knocking. She just tried the door and it swung open. She let herself in.

Shelly motioned for Abby to follow. Percy was kind enough to hold the door open for them.

"Thank you, kind Sir." Shelly offered in tithing before she entered the home.

The inside was immaculate, which seemed unusual to Shelly, considering the condition of the outside. The walls were paneled with wood up to Shelly's shoulders and elegant grey floral wallpaper. A staircase led to the upper floor but it was currently blocked by a red velvet rope. An "Off Limits" sign hung from it.

There were several rooms, all closed off by thick wooden doors and a red carpet that lead up to an oak desk. Behind the desk, sat a pale teen with shaggy brown hair in an oversized suit jacket. He watched them suspiciously as they came in. He looked like he was in 10th grade.

As they approached, the boy brought his hands up in front of him, revealing that his sleeves were far longer than his arms. He took out a pair of glasses, gave a fake smile, and put them on to greet them. "Good morning."

Lydia waited a few seconds in anticipation of some kind of follow up. When nothing surfaced, she sighed heavily, took the invitation from her pocket and placed it firmly on the counter.

"I received an invitation." Lydia stressed.

"Did you now?" The boy picked it up, opened the envelope and looked it over very carefully. "Are you sure it's from here?"

"Of course, I'm sure. I just gave it to you... are you saying that I wasn't supposed to be invited?" Lydia offered, quite cross.

"Not at all, Miss Grouchy." He weighed it in his hand and then tossed it in the air a few inches to test how it was affected by gravity. "It's always good to check for counterfeits."

"Counterfeit!" Her voice filled with venom. "It's an invitation. By appointment only at 10 a.m. It's now 10."

"I suppose it is." He put the invitation back inside the envelope and slid it back to her. "Welcome to the SOK Market. What can I do for you?"

Shelly spoke up in hopes of avoiding a potential catastrophe. "Actually, we have questions."

Lydia pointed at Shelly. "You! – Zip it!" She

barked with a snap of her hand. "I was here first, so wait in line."

Her hand dove back into her dress pocket and she replaced the envelope with the patch. "I want to know what you did to my brother."

The desk attendant leaned over to look at the patch she had acquired from the night before but didn't touch it. He looked up at her. "I didn't do anything. You must have done something pretty harsh in order to get that."

"Stop playing around." Lydia demanded. "My brother was fine two days ago. Yesterday morning he fell ill. Then he went crazy."

The boy didn't act surprised. "How old was he?"

"Seventeen." She replied.

"Are you sure? Did he have a birthday or something recently?"

Lydia thought for a second. "18 – I guess yesterday was his birthday."

"Bingo!" The boy announced while simulating a gun with his finger, for which he had to pull back his sleeve to show her.

"What Bingo? You can't just say Bingo."

"Of course, I can."

"And why is that important?" She sassed.

"Because once you turn 18 you become a monster."

"That's not funny." Lydia angrily remarked.

"I'm being serious. That's the rule." The kid reinforced as he crossed his arms.

"Since when? Whose rule?"

"Since yesterday, and I can't tell you who made the rules."

"Can't? Or won't?"

"Both."

She sighed. "What's so special about yesterday?" Lydia asked with further distaste.

"You don't know? All the parents are gone. The rest of the adults are gone too. Everyone above the age of 18 are in the wind and they're not coming back. Everyone who's left has received their prize and are on their own."

Shelly interrupted again. "What do you mean by, 'prize'?"

The boy hovered his sleeve over the patch on the counter. "Everyone has a patch." He smiled. "That's how you got this one. It's your brother's. I'd keep it safe, if I were you. You can't just leave it lying around."

Abby managed a peep. "What do you do with it?"

His smile widened. "I'm glad you asked. Anything patch related, you come here to the SOK Market. We can store it for you. We have a rather large vault. But..." He trailed.

"But what?" Lydia asked with a hand on

her hip.

"It's not the safest place. It's certainly not where I would keep it."

"Where would you keep it then?" Thomas asked intrigued by his sales pitch.

"I'd make sure that no one could get it, not even my best friend." He pulled out a needle and thread from behind the counter and pulled back his sleeves. "I'd have it stitched on."

"That's stupid." Lydia pointed out with an upturned finger. "People could just steal your clothes."

"Oh-no," He reassured. "No-no-no, I don't mean your clothes. I was referring to your soul."

"Huh?" Abby blurted out.

"Come again?" Shelly expelled as if she hadn't heard him correctly.

The boy was quick to explain. "It's no big deal. It's kind of like a tattoo. It won't hurt, not too much, just a few stitches and it'll be all over. It's really interesting how it's done. You won't believe where your soul hides. Go on, take a guess. Where do you think it is?"

"Your heart?" Abby asked.

"That was my guess, but we are both wrong."

Catching onto the game, Thomas pointed to the side of his head. "Your ears?"

"No one has guessed that. But nope. Good

try. 'A' for effort."

Percy lifted up his foot. "In your feet?"

"No—not even... wait, yes! Leave it to a rabbit to get it right." The boy explained as he removed his glasses in salute.

Lydia sighed with impatience. "You have to be joking."

"I wish I were. I thought any of those places were just as good, but the truth remains, your soul rests in your feet."

"I hate to interrupt—" Shelly evoked with determination.

"Why? You've been doing it this whole time." Lydia pointed out in irritation.

Shelly ignored her. "Why do we have these patches to begin with? Who took our parents?"

"Notice how you went immediately to, 'who' took your parents instead of 'where'. That's very paranoid of you. But because I like you I'll be as truthful as I can, I don't know who, what, how or where your parents are but losing someone so important leaves a hole in your soul. It can hurt so bad that it makes you sick for days – weeks even. In some cases... years. That's where the patches go, they fill the gap that takes the pain away. Someone or something knew the pain you'd go through and kindly stitched you up. Probably happened while you were sleeping."

"So..." Lydia thought aloud. "If I had you stitch this to my soul – what do I get?"

"Oh, it wouldn't be me. It would be Mindy. Each patch has its own power." The boy put his hand over it and his eyes flashed with light. "This one allows you to eat anything and never get sick. You can even take on properties of what you eat... if you wanted. You eat a rock, you become rock. Get it?"

"Will it turn her into a monster?" Thomas asked with an edge of worry.

"Not unless she eats one." Said the boy matter-of-factly.

"Can I change back? I'd hate to become a sandwich just because I'm hungry." Lydia inquired.

"Of course you can change back. Otherwise this would be a really dumb power. I wouldn't even recommend it. This one..." he turned it over in his hands. "I fully endorse it." He set the patch back down on the counter and looked at his nails. "Anything else? Although I've really enjoyed our talk, I'm really busy today and there is the next appointment."

Shelly shook her head. "I don't think this is a good idea, Lydia."

"Well lucky for you it's not your choice. I'll do it." The blonde expressed with a hint of excitement. She swiped the patch off the counter. "Tell whoever it is that I'm ready to do this."

"You got it." The boy revealed a small brass bell from beneath the counter and rang it a few times.

Chapter 13

It only took a moment for a petite brunette, about Shelly's age, to emerge from a side room. She wore a black dress and had her hair pulled back in a bun. A pair of silver scissors hung from a chain around her neck. Her voice was deeper and scratchier than expected.

"This way." She motioned to the door she had emerged from.

Lydia stepped towards her and asked, "Can I bring someone along?"

The girl shrugged her shoulders. "I suppose. Just one though. There's not a lot of room."

"Fine, then." She stated, partially annoyed. "Thomas, stay here with Abigail. Shelly is coming with me."

"Me?" Shelly asked in shock.

"No – the other Shelly. Stop wasting time and hurry up."

Shelly grumbled a little, but followed after.

"Good luck." Abby shouted as they disappeared behind the door.

The room was long and rectangular. There was a dentist chair near the door with a table next to it. On top of the table was a needle and silver thread. On the far opposite wall there was a large red pin cushion. Oddly, there was nothing else.

"Liar. There is plenty of room in here." Lydia remarked.

Mindy shut the door. "You'd be surprised." She replied coldly.

The small girl walked to the table while Shelly and Lydia remained by the door. She picked up the needle and thread.

"You need to lie down." She pointed at the chair with her free hand.

Lydia took in a long breath of air before approaching the chair. She then sat down and smoothed out her dress. "How much is this going to hurt?" She asked with hint of nervousness.

"Lots." Mindy replied coldly.

"How is this going to work, exactly?" She inquired with more sharpness to her voice.

"Better I just do it." Mindy pushed on the toes of Lydia's shoe like testing a tomato. She reached out her hand. "Give me your patch."

Lydia had been clutching it the entire time and she paused before releasing it into her hand.

Shelly began to suspect that Lydia didn't want to do this after all and she was just putting on a face. Knowing her, she never knew when to back down.

"You don't have to do this if you don't want to." Shelly offered with as much sincerity as she could muster. "You could think about it – I mean, it's just yesterday that we—"

"Shut up, Shelly." The blonde tried to stare her down. "I'm doing this."

Shelly grew angry. She thought about leaving. Had it not been for her curiosity she would have. For some reason Lydia wanted her to see this. Wanted to show how tough she was, not to mention how she always felt the need of being first. This was something that Shelly couldn't compete against.

Lydia sunk into the chair. "Let's get this over with."

Mindy pulled a pair of tinted goggles out of her front dress pocket and fit them over her eyes. She brought the needle in front of her and concentrated on it. Within a blink, it radiated an array of prismatic colors. Then, without warning, Mindy stabbed the bottom of Lydia's foot.

Lydia yelped and her eyes widened with the pain. Tears streamed from her eyes as her body stiffened. Despite it all, she didn't move.

Mindy twisted the needle inside her, pulled it out and rushed to the other end of the room with a shimmering ribbon of light dancing behind her. She stuck the pin into the cushion and started examining the cloth-like strand.

Shelly couldn't take her eyes off it; it was

bright, and it hurt her eyes just to look at it. No wonder she had tinted goggles, looking that close would probably burn her eyes out of her sockets. It was beautiful, as colors fluttered about and sparkled. As it waved, Shelly swore she could hear the faint chiming of bells.

Right away, Mindy pointed to a gap in the light, a dark spot hidden among the folds. The tiny girl set to work immediately, threading the needle, placing the patch and then stitching it to cover the darkness.

Lydia no longer showed a torturous face, but appeared pale and frozen in her stare. Her hand twitched and her fingers kept trying to reach out for Shelly.

She felt bad for her, Shelly couldn't imagine what she was going through. It was both wondrous and frightening at the same time. Lydia would probably make fun of her later, but the only thing that she could think of was to hold the girl's hand. Lydia's fingers clutched into hers as hard as she could muster.

Mindy stitched the patch into place with a quickness that was hypnotizing. When she was done, she snipped off the excess with a pair of silver scissors that she kept around her neck. Mindy then pointed to a patch closer to Lydia's foot so that Shelly could see.

123

"That's her first one." She instructed with a lifeless voice. The patch resembled an ancient Egyptian eye. "That's a good one."

Shelly was going to ask her what she meant, but Mindy turned her back to her, returned to the pincushion on the wall, and slid the ribbon off the needle. The light snapped back into Lydia like an elastic band and she took a deep breath as if she had been holding it the entire time.

Lydia coughed a few times, causing Shelly to release her hand. She sat up as if the bed were on fire. A chill went down her spine.

"Are you okay?" Shelly asked out of concern.

Lydia glared at her. "What do you think?" She pushed herself off the chair. She sharply addressed Mindy. "Are we done?"

"We're done." She said as she took off her goggles.

Without words or thanks, Lydia left the room and returned to the entryway where everyone else was still waiting.

"How did it go?" Thomas beamed with a smile.

"Is everything okay?" Percy asked with a twitch of his ears.

"We're leaving." Lydia snapped back.

She grabbed Thomas by the hand and continued towards the door.

Percy was quick to follow after. "Are we not going to say goodbye?" The rabbit asked as they crossed the threshold.

"Have a nice day!" The boy yelled from behind the counter with sarcasm.

The door slammed behind them, causing both Shelly and Abby to cringe.

"I'm sorry." Shelly exhaled from the ordeal. "I don't think I got your name."

He thumbed to himself. "Arthur Rendie." He then uncurled a finger to the door. "Now, if you please leave, I have a lot of work to do."

So much for having him accept her apology. Shelly could not help but feel that Lydia was somehow tricked into something.

"Are we going now?" Abby asked with caution. "Because this place is really weird."

Shelly nodded and the two of them exited the house as quickly as they could.

Shelly explained what happened on the way. By the time they reached the corner grocery store Abby was all full of questions.

"So let me get this straight, you actually saw her soul? And it wasn't all evil looking?" Her cheeks beamed jokingly.

"No." She giggled, "Surprisingly. On the other hand, it was the first soul that I've ever seen so I don't really have anything to compare it to."

"That Mindy girl though, do you think she put our patches on? Just thinking about someone creeping into my bedroom at night and taking my soul out is frightening."

Shelly shook her head. "I don't think so. I mean, she could have, but I'm not sure."

"That Arthur kid, he certainly is a character. He seemed very interested in getting Lydia to put it on. What's his angle?"

"His angle?" Shelly laughed as she tried the doors. "Dang... locked."

"Yea – like what's in it for him? Who told him to do what he's doing? He's got to know something."

Shelly's hand remained on the handle of the glass doors. "It's obviously not being polite. Something's up."

"I don't even want to talk about the house."

"I don't think we're going to have much luck getting in." Shelly remarked with disappointment as she returned her hand to her side. The grocery store would have to wait.

"Phooey. I might have some things in my house that are still good. I'm sure we can gather them up and bring them over to your house."

Shelly flicked her ponytail behind her. "You don't want to stay at your house?"

"I don't think anyone should be alone through this."

"What do you think about pasta for lunch?" Shelly asked as she picked her bike back up off the sidewalk. "We have some pasta sauce in the cupboard."

"We did skip breakfast." Abby reminded herself as her stomach growled. She patted her stomach. "Let's get going and see what we can scrounge up."

They rode their bikes home.

Once they turned on Shelly's street, they were quick to notice a group of children gathering in the center of the street.

"What is going on?" Shelly asked as she slowed her bike.

A small girl, a 1st grader, cuddled a teddy bear that was almost the same size that she was. Her hair was blonde and stretched all the way to her ankles. She turned to see Shelly and Abby.

"Hello. Do you have powers too?" She asked in a quiet voice.

Shelly gave a strange look, and then looked over the rest of the kids, all varying in age.

The eldest Mendoza girl, who looked about the same age as Shelly, wore a fluffy black dress with white trim, and held a parasol above her head to keep the sun off. Her hair was long enough to cover her ears, straight and finely brushed.

Her brother, who they saw the night before, waved at everyone before opening the blue car door from opposite the street and climbed inside. Seconds later, the driver's side door of the white vehicle next to his sister opened and he stepped out. Everyone there clapped for him and he smiled.

"Did he just—" Abby didn't finish her sentence.

"That's really cool!" An ebony-skinned girl said excitedly. She looked to be a 5th grader, she wore a purple dress and sandals as she ran up to the Mendoza girl. "May I please touch your umbrella?" She asked with her hands behind her back.

The girl nodded slightly and held the parasol out to her, careful not to expose her own skin to the day.

The 5th-grader reached her hand out and touched the umbrella. A swirl of bubbles collected in her other hand and grouped together to form a similar shape. Then, with a single pop, the bubbles burst and created an exact duplicate of the same parasol.

She giggled. "Now I have one too."

Shelly couldn't believe it.

The girl with the teddy bear called out, "My turn, my turn!" And her hair grew long, and it lifted her off the ground. She rose high above everyone by several feet and then her hair separated and walked like legs, which carried her to a high branch on a nearby tree.

She clapped her hands and everyone was truly amazed. "I did it! I got up here by myself."

A quiet Asian boy was among them, he appeared to be an 8th grader. His hair was short and he wore a baggy blue shirt, jeans and sneakers. He whistled. It was normal at first, but it grew in volume and soon it was all that everyone could hear.

Shelly's head felt light and her stomach turned. Everyone else was having a hard time of it as well, as many kids put their fingers in their ears to block it out. He stopped before it got any louder than that.

Abby massaged the inside of her ear with her finger to express her distaste. She rotated her jaw a few times to pop her ear drums and then gave the thumbs up that she was okay.

"Your turn." The girl in the tree demanded cheerfully to the Mendoza sister.

She nodded happily. "Step back, Javier." She warned her brother.

He did as she told him to. She stretched out her hand, snapped her fingers at the car and it immediately turned to ash. The ash whirled up into the air like a cyclone and was sucked into her ears like a vacuum. In moments, the car was no more and there was nothing left to indicate that it was ever there in the first place. She then turned and snapped her fingers towards the center of the street away from everyone else and the ash poured back out of her ears and recollected into the shape of a car. Seconds later the ash disintegrated and the car was whole again.

"Whoa." Shelly said from all the weirdness. She was dumbfounded.

"What can you do?" The Mendoza girl asked with a Mexican accent.

Abby shook with elation. "This is so awesome! I'm going to show off, okay Shell?"

"Ah-erm, da... yea sure." Shelly tried her form a decent sentence. "Go ahead."

The freckle-faced girl set her bicycle on the ground and hustled over to the car. She pointed at it with a huge smile and commanded, "Up!"

Like the times before, the vehicle lifted off the ground. All the children let out a cry of awe as it floated in the air. Abby touched it lightly and it started to move, twisting slightly as it levitated above the street.

"Wow." Said the Asian boy. "That's really something."

The girl in the purple dress spun her

parasol over her shoulder and cast Shelly a joyous face. "How about you? What can you do?"

"Oh, you all are in for a treat!" Abby complimented. "Shelly's got an amazing ability."

"If you give me a moment, I'll need to get my hoop." Shelly said. She held up her finger. "Just a minute, okay? I'll be right back."

She didn't wait for an answer. She ran her bike over to her house, set it on the ground and went inside. Shelly rushed into the kitchen and picked up her hoop where she had left it last night before returning back outside.

Excited to show off, she didn't realize that by the time she made it to the middle of the street that the group of kids had increased.

Shelly positioned the hoop around herself and then looked up to see if everyone was watching, but a familiar knot tied itself in her stomach.

"Is there something here you plan to cut in half, Whinny? Or are you just going to show them how bad of a throw you are?" Lydia stood next to Abby, her arms crossed over her chest. The color had returned to her face and so too did her sneer.

"I'm sorry, Lydia. Did you drop by to ruin everyone's fun?" Shelly combated.

"Ruin it? Please! It had to be fun first

before I could ruin it."

"What do you want, Lydia?" Shelly demanded.

"You're a day late, Whinny. It's time you stop stalling and we do what we were supposed to do."

"Oh, and what was that?" Shelly asked with irritation.

"You and I have a score to settle. It's time we raced."

"I don't know if you noticed, Gains, but I can run a lot faster now. There's no way that you can beat me." Shelly touted as she pointed to her hoop.

Lydia narrowed her arched eyebrows and tilted her head. "You sure about that? You think you can win – Wynn?"

"I don't think Lydia, I know." Shelly declared.

She straightened her head. "Then what's the harm? Tell you what, if you win, you can have Thomas until the parents come back. And if I win, you can never speak to Thomas again."

"But Lee-dee..." Thomas muttered.

Shelly looked to Thomas. "That's a stupid bet, Lydia. Why would you do that to Thomas? He's your cousin."

"That's the reason why, hot shot. I don't want you hanging around my cousin. You're reckless, you're dangerous and worst of all, you're you."

"I'm not going to race you for Thomas. It's dumb. You're just going to lose."

"Sounds to me like you're afraid." Lydia pointed at her. "Afraid you'll be embarrassed in front of everyone."

Shelly felt heat rising in her face. "Fine! If you want to lose so badly. Let's race."

"Perfect." Lydia smiled deviously.

She walked to the floating car, opened her mouth, grabbed the bumper and swallowed the vehicle whole. If Shelly hadn't seen it herself, she would have known it to be impossible. Lydia licked her lips and then shifted her stance.

Lydia twitched and her body turned to steel, her wrists and ankles sprouted tires, and from her ribs extended the exhaust. She dropped to all fours and her tires bounced on the pavement. Her face acquired the polish of chrome, her eyes were glass and appeared like headlights. Her nose became the grill.

She revved a hidden engine and the noise startled everyone. "What's the matter, Whinny?" Her engine roared even louder. "Afraid you don't have what it takes?"

Lights Out
No Parents. No School. No Rules.

The series continues with Book 2!

Visit us with your parent's permission at:
https://www.nrmbooks.com

Play the Game!
Make Friends. Build a Clubhouse. Save the World.

Make your own character and join the children of Applewood in your own homemade adventures. Pick up the tabletop roleplaying game today!

Visit us at:
nrmbooks.com

www.ingramcontent.com/pod-product-compliance
Lightning Source LLC
Chambersburg PA
CBHW071003120726
47910CB00004B/1360